TWILIGHT
OF THE
MESOZOIC MOON
AND OTHER TIME TRAVEL TWISTS

Brent A. Harris

To my family, friends, and everyone who pulled me along the way.

Cover by May Dawney Designs

"It was not an asteroid or comet, because it would have killed everything."

--Robert T. Bakker

"An asteroid or supervolcano could certainly destroy us, but we also face risks the dinosaurs never saw; an engineered virus, nuclear war, inadvertent creation of a micro-black hole, or some as-yet-unknown technology could spell the end of us."

--Elon Musk

"The fault is not in our stars but in ourselves."

--Will Shakespeare

Stories

Foreword

Humanity has within it a great capacity for wiping ourselves out.

As I write this, war has broken out from the invasion of a sovereign state. The whole world holds its breath once again as a madman poises his finger over the button that could make shadows on the wall of us all. While I'm hopeful for the future, there's a small chance you may never read this for one sole reason: we excel at using and creating technology, since the biblical rock swung by Cain, to harm our fellow man. And we do this more and more effectively with each new technological leap.

Science fiction is supposed to warn us against such things. Even the most hopeful of sci-fi offerings, *Star Trek*, came only after an Earthly cataclysm of such proportion that it left little choice for those who remained to unite in pursuit of the stars. It's my hope that we may join in such a pursuit, as equals, without that cost in bloodshed, or the loss of this planet to propel us off world.

But not on our current heading. We seemed destined to destroy ourselves.

It doesn't have to be this way. Enclosed within this collection are stories to warn us of the dangers of technology used… poorly. Like the hammer that's been used to bludgeon a neighbor instead of to build a home for the poor, technology has the capacity to feed the starving, heal the sick, and bring peace. If it's wielded in such a manner.

Many of these stories play with the concept of time. Time travel seems like a force for good. But even with the best intentions, it's probably not a good idea to travel to the past. Ray Bradbury warned us against this in his story, "A Sound of Thunder," which has had a profound influence on my work. A single, literal misstep created unfathomable change. Similarly, *Back to the Future* warned us of the dangers of knowing what the future has in store. But let us stop to consider: It's not revisiting the past or unlocking the secrets up ahead we should concern ourselves with. Rather it's the choices we make now.

Like many of the time-travel twists contained within, our characters tend to find this out: either just in time to save humanity, or just a moment too late as the realization — and doom — washes over them like rays of sun over an empty wasteland.

While the goal of any writer is to entertain, and indeed I hope these stories serve that vital purpose, let these tales also serve as a Pandora for a brighter future, and not as another roadmap to destruction. If an author warns that The McGuffin Machine is a marvelous way to kill everyone, then let us hope we have the strength within ourselves from turning such a device toward destructive, violent delights. And instead, let us use the proverbial hammer to build ourselves up.

Shattered Moon

A Prequel to Twilight of the Mesozoic Moon

Gon' of tribe Rak, thought the notion absurd. There was no way the moon could simply fall out of the sky. The god who had made the moon his realm would not permit such a thing. In fact, sixty-six million years ago, he had shielded the Earth from cataclysm, intercepting an asteroid six miles long. The moon fissured, its orbit slowed and the god who dwelled there was reborn as the god of Two-Faces. For his sacrifice, Gon'rak's feathery brethren had been saved, evolved, and spread their civilization across the Earth.

The moon hung bright in the sky. Cracked and cratered, it was obvious to all creatures the Two Faces embedded in the surface, one on each side of the cleft. Two sets of eyes, two snouts, two mouths filled with neat rows of short, sharp teeth, and the faintest visage of plumes completing the eerie effect. One God bathed in light, the other in the shadows of the scar. The Two-Faced God ruled over them all.

And Gods do not fall. Right?

But the raptor-like dinosaur at the center of the concrete room had assured Gon'rak that the moon was doomed. He wasn't some unwashed heretic who would soon be whisked away by Imperator Soldiers. He was an Overseer, a direct spokesperson for the Divine Imperator Rex, and therefore it was news straight from the Gods themselves.

The Two-Faced God, through the snout of the Overseer, was telling Gon'rak, an insignificant pilot with a blemished record, that they were dying. That the future of his world was not up to the actions of fates and stars. It was up to him.

All Gon'rak had wanted, before being called into this emergency meeting, was a good bite to eat and some spiced blood to wash it down. Now, he doubted he'd be snacking on anything anytime soon.

He sat, stomach churning, in a typical drab, grey room of stone and cement in some non-descript office. It was like every other room in all the official government buildings which countlessly dotted the cityscape. It wasn't much different than his own barracks, really. What made it stand out, however, were the bright white and black plumes of the Overseer. They were the colors signifying the rank and station of someone much, much higher than Gon'rak had ever been in a room with.

His feathers ruffled. The Troodon he had snatched for Moonrise so many hours ago felt as if it had lurched back to life inside his stomach, clawing its way out. He longed for any view of the moon, for any reassurance that it still shone high. But the bunker was windowless.

Gon'rak tried to breathe but he choked on the air instead. He coughed through his nostrils which echoed loudly across the room. His fore-toes clacked subconsciously on the floor.

"As I was saying," the Overseer ignored Gon'rak's plight, "The Two-Faced God has spoken, and in their wisdom, they have created a plan to ensure their survival and in turn, our own."

Gon'rak narrowed an eye toward another pilot, the only other one in the room with them. He was larger, fiercer-looking, almost twice Gon'rak's size, with a more tapered, sharper snout and longer, crescent talons. Gon'rak's plumage slinked downward. He couldn't remember the pilot's name, only that he was stationed on the Western Shores, far away from here. That must mean the other pilot was good. Good enough to shuttle him all the way out here to the Eastern Capitol City of Theros.

The name hit him even as Gon'rak's feathers fell lower. Max' of Tribe Ron was said to be the best pilot under the moon – better than Gon'rak himself (notwithstanding the blight in his file). Certainly, Max'ron's tribe was superior. If it wasn't for the presence of the Overseer, then Max'ron would have been the most interesting and elevated dinosaur Gon'rak had ever met. He was setting all sorts of interesting records today.

Max'ron's people were a tribe so old and wealthy that they could wear their natural burnt red-orange feathers proudly upon their breasts rather than having to dye them as others, such as Gon'rak, had to do in the approved mottled greys and whites representing their lower stations.

Max'ron made no move. He sat, stoically and silently, soaking in every word spoken by the Overseer. Where Gon'rak's guts trembled, Max'ron remained a bunker, not unlike the room they were in. His look lingered too long. Max'ron snapped his neck toward him and growled. Gon'rak lowered his head. He lacked the privilege of his peer. Only his prowess as a piloted had even permitted him this opportunity to be here. But *here* was suddenly the last placed he wanted to be. Perhaps he could use this social misstep to excuse himself?

The Overseer hissed a rebuke and spoke with staccato toe-taps and guttural growls, getting back to the matter at hand. "The moon is failing. The Two-Faced God calls upon a pilot to lead their chosen to safety. You will both be trained. But, in the end, They shall only choose one."

Gon'rak had no issue with leaving the planet. Becoming a pilot wasn't his first choice, but it had allowed him escape. Escape from his family, escape from his failings. The feeling of flight was freeing. Leaving was fine with him. And if the Earth truly was doomed, then all the better. It was a crowded, disease-ridden, brutish place that had offered him nothing but anguish from that day long ago when—

The door to the office breezed opened and Gon'rak feathers ruffled with a new kind of feeling when he saw her. The air from the adjacent room rushed in, bringing with it a pheromone he'd not noticed so strongly since his journey from hatchling to tribe's male had begun. The fragrance she carried as she graced into the room suddenly called into question everything he hated about this place.

The Overseer introduced her, "This is Car'ren. She oversees the project and will take over the briefing and your training." Gon'rak noted irritation in the Overseer's toe-tapping. It wasn't custom for a female to be in charge. Gon'rak himself was surprised. But tonight had sent all sorts of surprises his way. What's one more?

Anyway, his attention was all on Car'ren, whose feathers, though plain and in accordance with the less attractive sex, was more than made up for by her scent. It carried traces of fern leaves after a rain and molasses freshly tapped by the pecking of humming Ornithos. It swept across his snout, fluttering and dancing like a feather caught in a light, warm breeze. His eyes met hers, those brilliant black onyx pearls cut by copper irises, sweet and full, like the wide eyes of a Compy chasing after prey. She did not look away, nor growl at him like the other pilot, even though her title was above the both of them.

Gon'rak resolved to do whatever it would take to beat out Max'ron and pilot the ship that would carry Car'ren and him to safety, off the world that had been ruined far before any god had had a chance to destroy it.

***

The simulation center was anything but the austere government grey. It was messy, and chaotic, as if a Triceratops had trampled the inside of an electronics shop. The floor – metallic grating – appeared to be hastily added to cover wiring and electronics that had not been designed for such stress testing. Wires, wrapped in bundles, hung like ribbons, across the room. The room was bathed in a soft, red glow while moisture condensers sprayed out a fog to keep their dander down.

His ancestors lacked the fine feathers he had, Gon'rak reminisced. He often thought of the past. And how things could have been different. In another life, where Gon'rak was free to choose his path, he had wanted to be a bone-digger. In his mind, large, Mesozoic monsters loomed above him, reminders of the past, or possible omens of the future.

But the Imperator didn't like those who reminded him of their savage ancestry – or the fact that their beastly ways had changed very little. The feathers had changed, their claws had grown to become opposable, but their teeth – and hunger – remained the same.

Two-Faced God had other plans for Gon'rak. Always at war, Theros, their home, needed pilots. And so it was that Gon'rak found his calling. Now, here he was, slotting his tail into the space allotted in his chair. The seating was different for this craft. Most notably, he faced upwards, toward space. But the usual controls were in place. There were two sets of steering and navigation controls, one at his feet for his claws and another for his hands and more maneuverable thumbs – a feature his ancestors lacked well into the last couple million or years or so.

Two others walked in, ignoring Gon'rak as they headed directly for a console at the front and right of the shuttle. They thumbed controls that lit up monitors around them. Each had identical plumes of a purplish tint, a rare enough tribal color that he could not place it. And the two, odd as they were, worked in tandem, operating disparate panels as one. Twins, he determined.

Some lever or button they'd pushed made the room shudder. Gon'rak twisted his mouth as the simulator cranked unexpectedly with life. Of course, caught off-guard, he lacked all composure when Car'ren swept into the room, her eyes directly on him.

"Good moonrise." She cocked her head oddly at Gon'rak and then caught the eyes of the twins, and then to someone at the rear of the room who Gon'rak hadn't noticed. Looking back, he saw it was the ship's captain, to which he had failed to display any honorifics. He slunk into his seat. The night just kept getting better…

Captain Gno'res stood, at the back of the ship, short and stumpy, but with the air of a Theros more into duty than titles. He nodded at Gon'rak and said no more of the mistake. "I hope you all have rested well," the captain growled lowly. "For there will be little of it to offer in the upcoming week, I assure you."

Gon'rak swiveled his chair around looking for the second pilot. He was missing. A momentary flutter of hope filled him only for it to come crashing down when he realized that there was just the one pilot's seat.

"You'll be taking turns," Car'ren said, cementing the sudden sinking in his stomach. Gon'rak had only this slim chance to make an impression. He'd no doubt Max'ron would make no mistakes. Like Gon'rak had so many years ago—

A monitor switched from showing a data read-out to an image of a ghostly red moon, with a thin glowing fissure running like a river across its surface. This, Gon'rak knew, separated the moon into two faces, the Two-Faced God.

Car'ren began her briefing with, "Our moon is cracked."

Gon'rak sighed. He knew that. Anyone who could look up could see. Meetings were tedious and full of the obvious.

"What you did not know, and could never be told," Car'ren continued, "was just how deep the fissure is and just how loosely our moon is held together. The damage done by the asteroid sixty-six million years ago was catastrophic. Only, it's taken all this time for the moon's slowed orbit to erode to this point of calamity. Make no mistake. If the moon falls, it will bring about the extinction of all life."

The room went silent. Not even a breath emerged.

A black, starlit picture emerged on a large monitor in front of them. The moon came to view. Yet, it took Gon'rak a solid moment to realize he was looking at it from the view of space. The moon was larger and in greater detail than he'd ever seen it before. From this point of view, there were no gods there.

From behind the moon came floating pieces of icy rock, a swarm of small shadows speeding toward the surface, like a swarm of mosquitos out for blood.

"As tenuous as the moon's orbit is, we believed it was likely to sustain itself for another thousand years or more. Until this—."

The screen zoomed in on a single asteroid, slightly larger than the rest, but still relatively small, hurtling itself toward the moon.

"A massive meteor shower, harmless to Earth, now threatens the balance. A strike by this single bolide will devastate the moon. As its orbit further decays, the moon will begin to separate and shatter from the forces of Earth's gravity. As it descends further, the moon will fall… and destroy this planet."

An image appeared, computer rendered but eerily life-like, showing the computer projections and model as Car'ren described. While the inhabitants of Earth were of little concern to him, the planet itself didn't deserve such an end. Gon'rak looked away.

"This relatively tiny space rock, much smaller than the asteroid that struck our moon, will finish the job that was started before our ancestors had even gained sapience."

Gon'rak hissed, causing everyone to stare. He shied away, like a ceratopsian caught with its mouth too full of grass.

Now, it was more important than ever that he fly the ship, full of those the Imperator had deemed necessary, no doubt, to wherever it was that would provide them safe harbor. At least, he assumed that was the plan. But judging by the cockpit's small size… he wondered how much time they had to evacuate and who would be coming with them. Or if that was even the plan at all.

He found his throat scratchy and voice faint under his toe-clicks as he spoke up, "And when will this happen?"

Car'ren replied, her voice low and sad. "The shower has already arrived."

***

Car'ren further explained that the Two-Faced God, in its dance with Earth, was unusually close. It hung like a dominating tyrant in the sky, fissured and cracked; its Two Faces scornfully admonishing everyone below with a deep, red crimson glow that reminded Gon'rak of the color of blood. It was already wreaking havoc on the coasts by causing erratic tides and coastal flooding, she'd said. It would only be a matter of time before their peninsula would face the same threats.

Gon'rak sat frightened by her words yet still captivated by her. It was like looking at a venomous spider and her elegant spinning; beautiful and dangerous. He lost himself in the imagery so deeply, he didn't hear her call his own name repeatedly.

"Gon'rak," he thought he heard her say. But the word meant nothing to him. He thought of his father and of his classmates from the academy. He thought about the places he'd been and the Theros he'd met. He thought about his favorite watering hole. He remembered all those people and places and with a decided sense of nostalgia, that they were already gone.

Captain Gno'res barked an order, which snapped Gon'rak to attention. His feathers ruffled, and tail twitched as he found the controls that would prepare the simulation to start and the ship to launch. He grimaced, showing off rows of razor-edged teeth. He stopped his thoughts and mentally ran through each button press and switch toggle before he began. As the pre-flight checklist cleared, the twins declared, in unison, "Ready."

Car'ren found her seat next to his. His tail twitched in response to her sudden closeness. Behind them, Captain Gno'res gave the command to engage shuttle launch.

Confidently, Gon'rak put his skills on display, initiating the start-up sequence. The rumbling below, even though it was all hydraulics, gave him a familiar sense of ease. On screen, monitors displayed that all was ready. So was he.

The simulator craft seemingly lurched forward; the large concave screen tricked his peripherally-based vision into sensing movement in combination with slight shifts of the craft on the gimble, like an amusement park ride. Everything was as smooth as a Hadrosaur's horn.

Curiously, a light on his console began blinking.

He stared at it. Warning lights seldom flashed when he piloted. His controls vibrated away from him. The whole craft rocked and shuddered. There was an imbalance to the craft that he'd not expected. As anyone who has piloted can attest, anything that flies must be balanced and buoyed – by a rigorous testing process that can last for months. If the numbers the simulator spat out were to be believed, this ship had undergone no such process. Something weighted the ship down, as if it had been bolted on as an afterthought. An alteration, whatever it was, could prevent the ship from flying, let alone rocketing into space—

He saw his error too late.

More alarms blinked. A klaxon blared from behind. The ship was crashing. Car'ren latched onto her control console and dug her toes into the grating. The twins up front did the same.

Violently, the ship spun wildly as he raced through every procedure he knew to get the ship back under his control.

It was of no use—

It was over too soon. The ship calmed, the monitors clicked off. And the red room brightened into white light.

Gon'rak kept composed. He prided himself on that much, though underneath, his anger and disappointment bubbled and burst like lava running under the surface of rock. He knew what had happened. He had killed them all.

Why was the ship weighted so oddly?

"It appears, we have crashed," one of the twins stated as a matter-of-fact. The other twin carried on, "and we've all died."

Car'ren frowned at him.

***

Deflated, Gon'rak tapped his claws outside the training room while Max'ron strutted in to take his place. It seemed as if days and days and a few eternities had gone by when in fact, the clock showed only three hours had elapsed when the Overseer brushed by him and into the room with a sharp growl. By then, his sharp talons had dulled into rounded nubs.

A few arduous moments later, the simulation doors hissed open. He could hear triumphant jubilation that carried on as Max'ron stood

19

at the doorway. Car'ren was beside the proud pilot, her feathers pressed against his as they squeezed out of the simulator together.

Gon'rak backed away from the group and took to a corner for shelter. He had botched his chance, not just with his own survival, but his chance to be with Car'ren. Death, by comparison, was such a slight thing.

The Two-Faced God promised pastures full of food and all the comforts of a giant nest. That was nice enough, if true. But Gon'rak had never given himself completely over to the gods. What faith he clung to had been faltering over the last few hours. Where were the Gods when he had most needed them? Afterall, the Gods vanished every month, only to return as a sliver of their former selves. So who could say what would really happen to him after death if the promises of the gods were just as fleeting?

But die he would, from a shattered moon, while Car'ren was carried away with Max'ron on the ship that he should have piloted.

***

The celebration was at a closely guarded watering hole in the cleaner, more protected part of the city. Gon'rak was surprised that the Overseer had let them out for the evening, and no matter how spoiled his mood was, he wasn't going to deny himself a chance to slip away from the compound and sip down some spiced mammal blood.

Trike's Place was empty, deliberately so. The Overseer wasn't about to risk an outbreak of panic from any of their loosened snouts from too much drink. Palms hemmed the place in, among natural and faux elements that gave the place a rocky, desert appearance, but for the stream circumnavigating inside, filled with fish and other consumables. Gon'rak had often hunted the lizards that occasionally poked out from holes in the rocky walls to feed on insects. A few lucky ones might dart back to safety in time. But tonight, the lizards were safe. He didn't feel much like hunting.

Gon'rak rested against a stone slab, eyes-wide at a pair of monitors. A storm raged against a coastal city he didn't recognize in some foreign country he didn't think he'd heard of before. News from outside their coasts was rare.

The screen clicked over to a Gliding event, and Gon'rak smiled. Though his species had never been able to fly, he often dreamed he could. The best athletes among them could glide and swoop for hundreds of meters. He wanted to be like them, more than anything. To fly away from any trouble. Maybe that's why he hadn't resisted his call to become a pilot.

The slow rhythmic scratching of music blasting across speakers, intertwined with sauropod bellows, helped ease his mind, as did the spiced drink. But not completely. It didn't help him ignore Max'ron's moves on Car'ren at a nearby booth. She didn't return any affection, but she didn't reject it either. His drink didn't help the day's events from gnawing at him either. And there was something else. The proximity to his childhood home…

His seat allowed him little comfort. Moving and stretching, restless, he rose, staggering one claw past another until he found his way to the door.

Outside, it was warm and humid and a breeze carried with it the usual seaweed and salt air of the ocean. It should have been a pleasant walk along the trails, but the further past the niceties of the clean street and the more he descended into the slums of the city, the more he guarded himself and snapped his snout at the throngs of nest-less scavengers.

He crept cautiously past a row of lodges, crowded and dirty. The running paths narrowed and darkened into alleys. Mud squelched beneath his claws as a low laying fog rolled in. Soon, houses gave way to hovels, and hovels gave way to nests made from whatever scraps could be weaved together. It seemed to Gon'rak as if Earth was doomed anyway, moon or no moon.

His thoughts drifted to a darker time, so long ago, when *his* world had become shattered. And soon he found himself wandering into the neglected neighborhood that had held so much pain.

Back to where his mother was murdered.

✳✳✳

Gon'rak believed, if only for a short while, that his absence had gone unnoticed. Surely, no one at the party followed him. And no one else, outside the throngs of Theros occupied with their midnight business, was with him now – except for the two Imperator Guards that stuck out like very rare flowers among the foliage. They hung back, but it was clear, due to their size and sharp claws, they could corral him at the time and place of their choosing.

Pressing the guards out of his thoughts, he made his way down the running trail to the coast, until he came across a barricade. A long fence of iron bars stretched into the distance. The fence was tall, too tall for most to jump over it, even though his species were astonishing jumpers. Gates at each alley were bolted by chains and locks. Large, diamond-shaped, reflective signs hung at intervals along the gate warned of biological hazards. Sentries armed with sharpened talons patrolled the path. He hadn't heard that the area was closed. It wasn't on the news and there'd been no mention—

Gon'rak's guards crept closer, until he was trapped on all sides. The sentries, curious by this new presence, puffed out their plume feathers and growled lowly. His heart raced. What had he stumbled into?

A claw landed on his shoulder.

Car'ren stood next to him. His heart, already pumping, beat faster. Where had she come from and what was she doing here?

It was strange. Despite so much madness in the world, she brought a presence of peace whenever she was around. Perhaps there was something in Theros worth saving, after all.

"Rough first day?" She spoke calmly, as if the calamity had been no more than an inconvenience. Maybe to her it was. But to a pilot…

"You followed me?"

"I didn't think it was wise for our star to be wandering the streets alone."

Gon'rak nodded toward the guard and sentries, who had multiplied since last glance. Though with Car'ren around, they kept their distance. He wondered what would have happened to him if she hadn't arrived. Some star.

"What brings you out here, alone?" Car'ren asked.

"Sadness," he answered, though he didn't understand why. It was stupid to reveal so lowly an emotion, least of all to her. Yet somehow, the truth just slipped out. He felt comfortable talking to her, like he had known her since they were both little nestlings.

"I wasn't raised much farther away," she jerked a claw back up a hill toward a neighborhood much grander than his. Maybe to her, it was modest. To him, that neighborhood was as unreachable as the stars. "Let's start walking back. We can talk more on the way. The guards will keep their distance with me around."

The pair moved through the foliage, under the shadows of the moonlight forest, as the other two raptors did indeed fall back.

"Why is the area secured?" He probably shouldn't have asked that. Questions were frowned upon.

"For you. It's for your safety," Car'ren said. She hesitated. "The real reason is disease."

Gon'rak reeled back. "The Overseers said those things were under control."

"That's what the media has been told. Really, it's a pandemic. We've always been plagued by diseases. Some of the most virulent strands we've found have lain dormant for millions of years. But with overcrowding, lack of sanitation, and access to clean water, they've resurfaced with a vengeance."

"That's not what the news reports."

"Do you really believe what your hear?"

He shook his snout.

"Right. It's why I picked you for this project."

Gon'rak's eyes narrowed. "Not for my service report?"

"Your evaluation is solid, but for one instance in your past. There are better pilots."

Gon'rak gave it some thought. After today's failure, he couldn't disagree. So what was it about him?

"Do you know how your mother died?" Car'ren asked.

Gon'rak stopped. "How do you know about that?"

"I did my research," Car'ren clicked. "I think it's why you've always been cynical of the Imperator."

"I'm not sure we should be talking about that," Gon'rak answered, feathers ruffling. They resumed their walk, though he cocked his head from side to side to see if anyone had overheard them. After a moment of stillness, he continued walking. His heart settled back down from its jump into his throat. "On her way back home from the hospital, where she worked, she was… murdered."

"Are you sure about that?" Car'ren asked.

He said nothing.

"Your mother didn't die from some random attack. She contracted the virus. She died helping others who were ill. The Overseers ignored the outbreak and covered up what couldn't be contained."

Gon'rak's feathers flattened, and his shoulders slumped. The world was indeed brutish and nasty. But who to blame now? Who was at fault for the way the Earth spun? Maybe it deserved to end – but with him off world to someplace better. Maybe by himself. He eyed Car'ren suspiciously. Who was she to know all this, and why involve him?

"I'm sorry, Gon'. Sorry for prying, sorry for your loss," Car'ren placed a claw on him tenderly, then began to dart back up the rise toward Trike's Place. Before she did, she said, "But your pain makes you perfect for the mission. For that, I've arranged another simulation run tomorrow. You'll have one last chance."

The words caught in his head, rattled around, and refused to come to any sense of order. What did she mean by that? And what had he done before, to warrant such attention? He tried to examine his past for any evidence, but outside of just being a decent pilot who had a slight tendency to kill his crew on their first foray out, the evidence came up lacking.

And now he'd learned that his mother had died, and the Overseers had hidden it from him, just as they were hiding the news of the planet's imminent doom. Gon'rak struggled with what to do with the information. Did it change anything?

No, he still wanted to leave. But to escape, he'd have to swallow his feelings over these new revelations and do just what they asked of him. Without question. Maybe they didn't need a great pilot. Just someone mediocre who could follow directions. He would just have to bury his pain.

He could do that. He'd been doing that his entire life. And if that was what it would take to sweep Car'ren off this doomed globe, so be it.

***

The second attempt at the simulation found an eager and exuberant Gon'rak, pacing quickly through the waiting room corridor, until he'd worn grooves from his blunted toe-claws into the flooring. Since he had failed so spectacularly, the Overseer had wished Max'ron to test first today, against an even more difficult simulation. Should he pass, there would be little reason for Gon'rak to fly. Clearly, Car'ren and the Overseer were at odds. To the extent of that fight, Gon'rak could only guess. But he reasoned that it had something to do with the overall mission and whatever was causing the imbalance of their ship. Where did Gon'rak fit in with all this?

As determined as he was, if Max'ron exited in the triumphant manner as before, his chance would evaporate before it even began. He had to be on that flight. Not only did he have questions to which he had no answers except through Car'ren, that ship was his only means of survival.

Hours passed like the creeping of eons once more. Gon'rak was starving, but too nervous to eat. His tail twitched, and his mind raced with manuals and start-up procedures, flight details, and the lingering question of why the ship was so poorly weighted. But now that he had a feel for the imbalance, he thought he could correct for it. Assuming of course, he could handle whatever else they threw his way.

The doors to the simulation room hissed open, and Gon'rak was so preoccupied with calculations that, while he noticed Max'ron exit the simulator, the pilot's shaking and tightly clenched snout did not register right away.

Absently, Gon'rak asked the pilot how it went.

Max'ron looked incredulous, as if Gon'rak had to be joking. All he managed to stumble out was, "Pounding… so much pounding," before the roar of the Overseer bid him to silence.

Gon'rak almost growled back, letting his simmering undercurrents whisk him to anger, but he remained in control and bowed like he'd never bowed before as he entered the simulator. He slid into his seat without issue and immediately ran through all his pre-flight operations.

Car'ren gave an encouraging smile from beside him as the Twins announced the system was ready and Captain Gno'res barked the order to engage launch procedures.

Gon'rak blasted off.

He minimized the rear inertial dampeners. Normally, this would have sent the craft careening out of control. Instead, the extra inertia exerted on the lower half of the ship gave him just a bit more control over the ship's ungainly upper end.

The ship flew smoothly, breaking atmosphere sometime later. Once it did, the simulation's computers compensated for weightlessness, Gon'rak switched the dampeners back on to full, and the whole ship glided effortlessly into the blackness like a Glider athlete back home twirling and sailing through the moon-beamed sky.

That's when the pounding started.

It was surreal at first, a sound that didn't belong in the quiet of space. It was like pebbles hitting a metal roof. Up north, he'd heard of hail and wondered if this was a similar sound.

"Captain, reports of damage to exterior craft," one of the twins called.

Car'ren kept her snout down at her controls, as if keeping to herself anything that might give the game away. Gon'rak tried to puzzle together the test before the captain interjected his thoughts with an annoyed, "Pilot, steer us clear."

Like an idiot, Gon'rak had not learned the names of the Twins, seeing as it was hopeless to tell them apart anyway. Instead of addressing them, he asked openly, "Could I get a viewscreen of outside, please?"

A moment later, darkness filtered into view, as distant stars dotted the screen. Pinpricks of dark shadows flicked past, in time with the thudding against the hull. A large, lighter shadow loomed over the whole scene. They were flying through the meteor shower on the dark side of the moon.

Gon'rak set to work. Calmly clutching the controls, ignoring each thud, he put the pounding out of his mind and flew a zig-zag set of obliques along a round-about course toward the indicator icon in the distance.

He felt alive again and welcomed the challenge. When a particularly large rock loomed ahead on the view screen, and his sensor screeched, he deftly barrel-rolled by it. But when another indicator light flicked to life, Gon'rak realized he had an impossible choice to make. Two asteroids, each large enough to obliterate the ship, threatened his path. He could only dodge one.

If he chose to hit the asteroid above, it would most likely destroy whatever equipment or device they were carrying – the godsawful device that had made the ship wobble and crash his first flight out. He surmised that it was important, that the Imperator, and the Overseers, and the Two-Faced God wouldn't want a single scratch on it.

He dodged it, and let the lower asteroid graze the bottom of their ship. They had dampening shields, but how much could they take? The ship shook. The twins nearly lurched out of their seats, saved by their latch-belts. He heard an audible "Oof" from the Overseer and grinned at that. A backward look revealed Captain Gno'res was unfazed, almost bored at the affair.

But it was Car'ren who took the worst of it.

Her control panel lit a fiery red-orange… and then went dark. She slammed a claw against her control panel.

"Captain, critical failure at the science station," a twin called.

Gon'rak just killed Car'ren.

"I can see that, thank you," the captain returned. "Pilot, can you get us to the target without killing any more of my crew?"

"Yes, sir," he said.

"Then, proceed."

Gon'rak didn't have a chance to consider what he'd done, though part of him felt ill. The rest of him was jubilant. He saw a path toward their destination and sat to work at the controls. He'd done everything asked of him and more. He'd even shown deference and respect to the damned Overseer. Still, the slumped figure of Car'ren, even if in pretend, tore at him. It wasn't just that he had killed her. Something in her body language, the way she faced away, told him that she was upset, but not for the obvious reason.

***

A while later, Gon'rak exited the simulator the same way Max'ron had done yesterday. The twins exploded with excitement adding to the praise from the Captain and even the Overseer himself. "You did a fine job, pilot. You've scored exceptionally well. The Imperator Rex would be proud to have you fly the mission."

It was Max'ron who soured and sulked off into a corner upon hearing those words. The only thing missing was…

Car'ren.

Where she had been cozy with Max'ron following his success, she was absent in the room now. As the others trailed off, including the defeated pilot, Gon'rak turned to find Car'ren glowering.

"You." Car'ren poked a rounded claw out. "I expected better from you."

"I'm sorry I killed you, believe me. But I don't understand. I fulfilled the mission. I did just what the Overseer wanted. Didn't you see how pleased he was with me?"

"Yes. That's exactly what happened." She lowered her head and made as if to leave. Gon'rak let her by, but before she left, she stopped and turned back as she had done the previous evening. "When I investigated your file, I saw something else. A blemish. It caught my eye. That's why I brought you in."

Now, Gon'rak was utterly confused. The only mark in his record was the one time he'd disobeyed orders. Yet, they clearly wanted an unquestioning follower, and that's what he'd delivered.

"You were flying a transport full of Imperator Soldiers. En route, a small civilian craft, whose guidance system malfunctioned, flew into your flight path."

Gon'rak knew this story well. He didn't want to be reminded of it. Still, he listened. It wasn't just the way she smelled that attracted him to her, there was something more, something he'd been blind to before. He respected her, he discovered, which made her dressing down of him more hurtful.

She carried on, "You, against orders, disabled the autopilot and risked the lives of everyone in your craft to avoid hitting the civilians. The smaller craft would have simply disintegrated against your transport's dampeners."

"Yes, and it served as a blight in my career ever since. No one wants a pilot who can't follow a mandated flight path."

"I did," Car'ren cried out. "I wanted someone who might just have an inkling of sense about themselves, someone who might," she lowered her voice, "question just what plans the Imperator Rex has for my invention. We're not just going into space; we're going back in—"

A klaxon sounded.

Gon'rak swiveled in alarm, sweeping his eyes across the room for the klaxon's source. The simulator was powered down. The room itself was silent.

"It's coming from outside," he said. "Could it be, is the moon beginning to—?"

"No, the Imperator has decreed that there is to be no outside warning for that. Only we are to know."

The news of that hit hard. Maybe Car'ren was correct… maybe he'd been wrong about everything this whole time.

Before he could think on it longer, realization struck harder. "The klaxon, that's a storm warning, for tidal swells and hurricanes—"

"You're right, we can help."

"You want us to race toward the storm surge?"

Car'ren answered by darting away. Gon'rak followed her, the pair racing onward against the gathering storm and rising tide.

***

Outside, there was no wind, no rain. Only the sudden swell of surf building up to batter the coast. The two of them were intercepted by Imperator Soldiers and ordered to safety at a bunker next to the full-sized spacecraft on a landing platform high up on the hill. This was the first time Gon'rak had seen the ship in the daylight. At night, it was shrouded by darkness.

The craft was surprisingly small. Certainly, it could not serve as an ark, shepherding teeming masses to a brave new world. It barely seemed large enough to fit their flight crew. The unfinished ship was oblong and white, and a strange, bulky contraption wrapped around it like a band. That strange ring must have been what weighed the craft down and made it nearly impossible to fly.

But what was it for?

Above the ship, the Two-Faced Moon hung pale as daylight faded, becoming angrier and more vengeful with each darkening stroke of the clock.

Down the hill, on the shore, the coast was threatened by a swelling tide, unchecked by even the strongest of their fortifications. He'd been there last night and saw the barricades. There were raptors trapped between the water and the quarantine zones. Families he knew from hatchlinghood. What would happen to them?

A while later, a stream of soldiers marched onto the hilltop, as the surf continued to rise. Waves increased in reach, sweeping their way further and further inland. Why were the soldiers marching to the hilltop rather than to help control the likely panic below?

"What's going on?" Car'ren demanded of the Overseer. "Why are the soldiers here?"

"I do not answer to females." The Overseer growled, then promptly ignored his own words. "This mission is of the utmost importance, and until the craft is complete, I will not see it endangered."

Gon'rak went up to Car'ren, concern stretching across his snout. His head cocked to one side. "What will happen to everyone behind the barricades?"

"Soon, our Gods will shatter, and everyone will die. It does not matter if their deaths come now or later." The Overseer spoke without a trace of empathy. "Our project is the only thing that matters. It is the will of the—"

"Don't you dare say it," Car'ren commanded. She shot Gon'rak a look of, "I told you so," and darted down the hill toward the city and the danger below.

"I don't think she likes you," Gon'rak said to the Overseer before he raced to catch up to Ca'ren.

The Overseer roared back, "If you leave the safety of this hill, you will be removed as pilot from this program."

He stopped in his tracks to consider the Overseer's words carefully. To stay meant safety. It meant continued life away from the ruined world. For generations Theros would know his name and speak it as a noble, perhaps, holy, word.

Gon'rak thought of his mother, and how she had died helping others and how all that had been hidden from him. His faith was no longer blind and Gon'rak found himself treading in dangerous waters all on his own. "What's the point of salvation if we aren't worthy of saving?"

Gon'rak did not expect to receive an answer. He didn't. So, he turned away to chase after Car'ren. Behind him, he thought he saw the flash of Max'ron's shadow.

***

"What exactly are we supposed to be doing?" Gon'rak called after Car'ren. They had to shout to be heard over the roar of crashing waves and panicked raptors weaving through the running trails, seeking higher ground.

"I don't know…," she sputtered. "Got any ideas?"

Gon'rak wanted to come up with a smart move. To show Car'ren he cared, not just for her, but for others. Just as he had done long ago to save the civilian plane that had crashed his own career. But he had no idea. He wasn't smart or clever. He just acted. He always had. So, he did. "Help those who can't help themselves. Find a way to open the gates."

They sprinted past Trike's Place, the watering hole now literally filled with water, toward the slums, to the barricades. Raptors were trapped between the quarantine fences and the swell of raging waters. They bit and gnawed at the great iron bars. Some wormed their way up rock ledges, or tall trees and attempted to glide over. Some made it, but not all of them, and they couldn't all escape in time. Water continued to rise. Their snouts looked hopeless. He could smell pheromones of desperation cloy the air as cries for help clawed his ears.

Car'ren pointed at the metal chains holding the barricades in each alley in place. "I need a bar of some sort."

"A what?"

"I just need something sturdy enough to pry the locks off—"

Gon'rak thought he understood. The water was cold as he splashed past several unhelpful, empty buildings. Branches were too thin or too wet, and palm fronds were useless. But, nearby, a single metal rod, the type used in construction of concrete buildings, stuck askew from out of the ground. It threatened to disappear beneath the water. He pried it free and brought it back to Car'ren. "Will this work?"

"It might not be strong enough, but it'll have to do." She jammed the bar into the midpoint of a weave of chains. Together, pressed wetly and tightly together, turning the bar repeatedly, until the chains tightened into a ball, the bars bent inward, and the weakest link gave way.

The gate popped open. Raptors crushed and trampled one another to escape the rising tide. The bar was lost under the stampede. Car'ren called, "Get another bar and work your way across the locks."

Gon'rak was soaked. His feathers wet and soggy, his wings were heavy and he could barely move. It was no use, Car'ren swam just as clumsily. They weren't built for swimming under water. It was all they could do to get to higher ground themselves.

They'd saved some of their kin, but others, likely those too sickly or small, and those too far from this opening, would die…

"We have to get back," Gon'rak said. "We have to help them."

"We can't." Car'ren was drenched. She shook her snout. It wasn't like her to give up. But from the ground, she pointed to something or some *one* behind him.

Max'ron towered over him, barring his way. His breath stank of blood and meat. He was flanked by two nasty looking Imperator soldiers, the same ones from last night.

"If I kill you, pilot," he glared, "I'll escape this awful world. I'll survive." Max'ron's vibrant red chest flared against the black waters swirling around them. He glanced at Car'ren. "And my tribe will flourish."

"Stop," Car'ren demanded. "My plan is for peace. You don't understand—"

Her words went unheeded. Max'ron lunged, aiming teeth and claws straight at Gon'rak.

***

Gon'rak's wings were too waterlogged. He couldn't move as fast as Max'ron. He took the lunge full on, but the surging water buffered the blow and Max'ron's claws were unable to gouge Gon'rak's flesh. And now, Max'ron was just as wet and slow.

"Car'ren, get back to the fence, help the others. I'll keep the big one busy."

The two Imperator soldiers hissed, encircling her. Car'ren spoke sharply, "You stop me, you hurt him, and I'll see your feathers plucked."

The guards looked at each other. They paused, unsure, but did not stop her as she leapt into the water. That was odd. If Max'ron was operating on his own, Car'ren's authority should have held no such sway. Something was off about this whole encounter. He'd have to figure it out, if he survived.

Max'ron bared his teeth, darting at Gon'rak's neck. Like a pilot flying a ship, Gon'rak barrel-rolled out of the way. He spun his right toe-claw up and dove down, aiming for Max'ron's abdomen, but missed.

Max'ron saw another opportunity to lunge and took it. Edges of his sharp teeth drew a thin line of blood and a mouthful of feathers. Gon'rak kicked hard once more, this time, his talon finding flesh. He flapped his wings hard, splashing and spraying salty water into Max'ron's eyes, and then plunged backward, putting distance between them.

Car'ren reemerged, clutching a pair of nestlings. Max'ron and the two soldiers stalked toward Gon'rak. Only this time, Car'ren couldn't save him. Behind them, a wave swelled, threatening to crash down and drown them all.

"This planet is doomed," Max'ron leapt into the air, aiming for the kill. "And the weak with it."

The wave started to descend.

"Everything ends," Gon'rak said. "What matters is what we do before."

He sunk his toe claws into the ground below, and braced, hoping Car'ren caught his cue to do the same. As both wave and claw crashed down over him, everything went dark.

***

When Gon'rak retrieved his senses, the waters were retreating into the ocean. The swells had reached their peak and were receding along with the moon's straining attempt at crawling across the horizon in its usual withdrawal.

Car'ren was soaked, clinging to safety as the nestlings clung to her, looking for all the world a hero. She smiled at Gon'rak, oblivious to his feelings for her.

The guards and pilot were gone.

Gon'rak scanned the water.

So did Car'ren. She pointed out a shape bobbing in the surface. "There, I think that's him."

Gon'rak considered letting Max'ron wash out to sea. But it hadn't been the pilot's fault. Some were more blind to the Imperator's control than others, just as Gon'rak himself had been. He swam as well as he could to the pilot and brought him back.

***

"I'm glad for your safety," The Overseer growled at Gon'rak once they were all returned to the hilltop aside the incomplete shuttle. "Of course, you realize that you're off the mission?"

35

The once normally unquestioning Gon' of tribe Rak would have stood in silence. This Gon'rak did not. In a tone laced with snark he said, "You ordered Max'ron to kill me."

The Overseer paid no heed to the obviously nonsensical claim. "He went nobly and heroically into the diseased infested slums to save Car'ren from your disobedience. You may be a better pilot, but we need someone who will follow orders."

"Of course," Gon'rak answered.

He gave his goodbyes to the captain, and then the twins. Turning to Car'ren, he remained impassive as she whispered, "Don't think for a moment we've seen the last of you. This project needs you."

He caught the subtext. Something deeper was going on here, he knew. And despite being off the project, he vowed to find out. He began to head back to the barracks before the Overseer stopped him. "Car'ren is correct. Should something happen to Max'ron, should the Two-Faced God will it, They will call upon you to complete our holy task."

"Right," Gon'rak grinned, as he darted away from the strange compound. There was no chance of that. He decided not to return to his barracks for now, but to head instead toward the city, to help where he could, for as long as he could, until the moon shattered, and his world ended.

End.

I'd been toying around with giving the bones of "Twilight of the Mesozoic Moon" some flesh in a fully realized novel. "Shattered Moon" was an attempt to play around with these characters to see what larger story there was to tell, if any. As such, this story isn't meant to stand alone (it concludes at the end of this collection for those of you who'd like to jump ahead). I'm not sure if a novel-length adventure for Gon'rak will happen anytime soon, but I hope an idea will click into place. For now, this prequel story is exclusive to these pages.

Now, for something completely different. A new "Twist" to a classic story that's been the bedrock of my writing for years. The short story that inspired a whole series of books: A Twist in Time.

A Twist in Time

Oliver twisted between rows of costermonger carts, each seller accosting him with wares he'd never be able to afford, each seller more desperate than the last. They reminded him that London was altogether strange territory in contrast to the quietness of the country. The noise alone was nearly unbearable.

"Pippins!" A gaunt gentleman pleaded to no one in particular, "Pipin' hot pippin pies!" Sidestepping that man, Oliver stopped just short of a mud pile that he was pretty sure wasn't mud. It didn't smell like it anyway and the streets were piled thick with it. He was almost past the last cart and down to the street when another dirty face shoved into his, "Get yer Yarmouth bloaters and whelks!" The smell of bad fish and rancid snails overcame the waste in the streets. Oliver stopped for a moment to wipe away tears and cupped a hand to his ear. Through the din, he caught his name.

"Remember, Oliver. Just like we practiced with the Old Man." Oliver caught sight of Jack, standing there in his oversized coat, sleeves rolled-up, looking decidedly in charge. Charley was by his side, pushing his hands forward as if he was egging Oliver on.

Oliver pressed forward, setting aside the twisting in his tummy from so much sneaking, as he made for his mark once more. He'd lost him for a moment in the busy street, as horse carriages passed them by, splattering what remained of the last rains and morning bed pans over the inhabitants of the city.

There. A dapper-looking, overly dressed gent, if ever Oliver saw one before. Jack called it, "butter upon bacon," a run of words that he didn't quite get.

"Fancy that tall top hat too, eh? The black one with the red quill," Charley added.

"That's your man. He's in on the game, but still, don't let him feel you poke 'im, right?" Jack warned, as he and Charley shoved him along.

As Oliver approached from behind, he caught sight of the prize. A tiny triangle of a silk square teased out of the gentleman's waistcoat pocket. He supposed that was his target. The room they let was full of them, and the Old Man often hid those about his person as Oliver, Jack, Charley, and rest of the boys played at trying to make a grab for 'em. Only, this wasn't inside their flea-invested hovel.

In between slow breaths of shallow air, Oliver eyed something that changed the game entirely: A piece of gold glinted in what little light the streets could catch. As he closed the gap between himself and the window-shopping gent, he could make out a pocket watch chain.

He could have sworn it looked similar to one he'd seen in the Old Man's hoard. If it was the Old Man's, then the gentleman with the fancy tall hat was indeed in on it. And Oliver could relax. The game he'd learned inside the crowded letting-room, was continuing out here on the streets. It was all for a spot of fun, wasn't it?

The chain wasn't even latched to the man's waistcoat. The pocket watch was just hanging there, as if to emphasize the point. It *had* to be a game. With a quick peep around for any extra eyes, he silently slid the watch out of the man's pocket and into his own. He'd done it the same with the Old Man and gotten coin and praise. Now, wouldn't the Old Man be proud?

But the watch felt heavy in his pocket. Heavier than anything he'd ever carried. The weight of it made him wonder if he should continue with the game and grab the handkerchief too. Something felt off.

The gent turned and walked away, his top hat tilting against the turn, leaving Oliver alone with his prize. He looked around, and it seemed no one had seen what he'd done, including Jack and Charley. Oliver held his prize within his pocket, thumbing its crown back and forth as the boys reached him.

"Didya do it? Didya nick him?" Jack asked.

"Nah, he ain't done it. I still see the handkerchief sticking out." Charley answered before Oliver could. "I told yer he ain't no prig."

"We'll make you one, good and proper, Oliver," Jack said, shaking his head. "Won't we? You'll be as good an upstandin' man as any. The Old Man says so."

"He's not ready."

Oliver said nothing, as he kept his hand hidden in the pocket with the watch. He'd give it to the Old Man himself.

"Oliver, just watch," Jack instructed, causing Oliver to jump at the word. "Watch professionals such as myself and Charley here instruct you again. Can't go home empty-handed now, can we? Not if we want to fill up on bangers and get half-ratted on gin, eh?"

The trio turned toward another corner and Jack pointed out a bloke buried in a book. "Look there, a man a world away, won't notice nuthin'. Come on, Charley. Oliver, get up real close, mind us, and mind for Bobbies."

The boys were already on the man, leaving Oliver thumbing the crown of his pocket watch. *What were they on about?* He almost answered his own question when a cry came from inside the bookshop. Jack and Charley had relieved the man with the book of his handkerchief.

Oliver knew he should run, but the weight of the watch kept Oliver cemented as Jack and Charley blended into the crowd and the bookstore owner exited the shop and called to the man, "You've been robbed!"

"Th-thief!" The man with the book locked his eyes with Oliver's.

He couldn't break away from the steely gaze. He was a thief. He had not stolen the man's handkerchief, but he stole the pocket watch.

Oliver bolted away, realizing that he wasn't running away from the crowd at the shop, but from himself. He glanced back and the man with the book gave pursuit, along with a throng of people – those in rags mixed with those in finery; all equal in their pursuit of the boy. Even Jack and Charley gave chase, laughing as if it were still a game.

They ran down the road. Only this time, Oliver did not check for the stink of the street, which splashed beneath his feet, soiling him. He did not dodge the carts, or their wares. Red pippins and yellow-green pears went flying as costermongers leapt away from Oliver and the crowd, some of them joining the pursuit in protest.

Was this to be his lot in life now that he'd thrown in with a criminal lot? He couldn't think about that with a mob chasing him. He didn't want to consider the noose, or other dark futures his fate might hold. He kept running, away from it all.

Oliver needed to get rid of the watch. He may be innocent of the handkerchief, but there would be no way to explain away such a hefty piece of jewelry. As he ran, he tore out the watch and took a hard sidelong look at the infernal devil.

The pocket watch was smooth, from what he could see, and the crown and the latch-button were where they should be. It looked like any other pocket-watch, plainer than most. But it was monstrously heavy now. It seemed to call to him, in short, sharp ticks. Louder now. It was all he could hear.

His fingers were fumbling with the watch, stuck on the latch button. It called to him, beckoning him to push the button. Oliver dismissed the thought. It was the mob behind him. Not the watch. He wanted to let it go, fling it far away, unseen, so they could not catch him with it.

He rounded the corner, and the watch seemed to vibrate, as if he could feel each gear click into place. Oliver almost stopped, but he was a tick ahead of the crowd and now was his chance to be rid of it. Yet his fingers still tangled on the latch, the chain wrapped around his hand. It wouldn't let go. He struggled with it for a moment when the latch popped and the cover flew open—

And then Oliver was alone.

Or rather, the distance put between himself and his pursuers was… impossible.

He was higher on the hill, the crowd of people below, chasing after someone who was no longer there. Every bit of him shook. How was he here? He didn't know what to think, but somehow he knew the watch was to blame. He made as if to throw it away.

Somewhere, in the background, the church bells of London rang, loud and clear through the streets, striking the cobblestones and bricks with deafening discord. When they stopped, Oliver's ears continued to ring. But through the din, he heard a new voice.

"If I were you, I'd keep the watch."

Oliver turned to see the man with the tall top hat. "Keep it until you're back, at least. I'll need it returned then, if you'll be so kind." The man smiled, and Oliver shook his head in astonishment.

"What?"

Oliver heard the mob from down the hill, "There he is!"

"You didn't go forward far enough from the looks of it. The crowd has seen you. Give the timepiece a turn, about a dozen, I should think. Just remember to turn it back the correct amount when you wish to return."

Oliver stared but did not move. The crowd was once again racing after him.

"Now's the time for haste," the man said, winking.

Oliver spent his whole life taking direction, living a life other than his own. Doing what others told him became reflex. But in this instance, he hesitated. Then the man nodded, a sincere nod, with a smile the likes of which Oliver had never seen before. He did as instructed.

First, Oliver closed the cover and twisted the crown, stumbling a bit over his numbers—he'd learned those with the Commandments. Oliver twisted through eleven and stopped when he reached twelve… or was it thirteen?

"Ah, that's a good lad. Keep to your innocence while you are there. And remember the bells when you return. I'll see you in a moment."

Oliver looked at the man, then turned toward the crowd. He saw them rushing toward him, Jack and Charley and the man still holding onto the book, along with more people than he'd seen stuffed in a small church on Sunday. They were heated and looked as if they all wanted Oliver to hang.

He gulped and flipped open the watch. And once more, he was whisked away. Only this time, he didn't land on a filthy London street.

Oliver was alone yet surrounded by more life than he'd ever known. Wide branching trees, perfect for climbing, enveloped him. The breeze blew crisp wind; the only foul smell was him. There was quiet hidden in the cacophony of the woods. It was a peculiar peace. Strange as it was to Oliver, it felt familiar, as if he'd found what he'd been searching for these last nine years of his troubled life.

Nearby, water churned. *A river!* If it was as clean and soft as the forest floor, as blue and bright as the air around him, Oliver wanted to see it, bathe in it, and leave everything behind. The last time he'd seen a river, it was the Thames, and he'd smelled the rotting animal corpses even before he saw them drift across it. Yet, that time was gone now, and this new land beckoned him onward.

He shoved the watch absently down his pocket, the urge to explore was stronger than the whisper of caution. The weight of it was gone. And Oliver bounced ahead, forgetting for a moment all his questions as to where and how he was here.

It was hotter than it was in London, much hotter, and his skin was already starting to feel sticky. It would be good to take a bath in the river. He could cool down, wash off, and then he could figure out what was going on.

He'd taken a few eager steps toward the river when the birds began to quiet. A flap of wings broke off from cover. In the soft sounds of the forest, he could hear something – and nothing. And that was when a girl crashed into Oliver, sending them both falling, tumbling toward earth.

They bounced down the hill, until they broke their fall in a bramble of bushes. Oliver could feel the watch slip out, as if the earth itself reached in and picked his pocket, just as Oliver did earlier.

"No!" Oliver lunged through the undergrowth, long thorns cutting through his rags and into his skin. A hand wrapped around his mouth and lips pressed against his ear.

"Quiet." It came out as a harsh whisper, ringing in Oliver's ears, but he paid no heed. The watch was too important. He struggled to his feet, even as another arm wrapped around him and pulled him back down. "Be still!"

The girl held him tightly, but there didn't seem to be anything mischievous in her grasp. If anything, Oliver sensed fear. "Let me go, I won't run," he told her in a hushed voice.

"Who are you?" the girl asked.

She was dressed in attire worse than Oliver's. It seemed like someone cut holes in an empty sack of flour and stuck it over her head. She was thin and starved, her dirt-colored hair pulled back and wrapped with a piece of plant. Oliver guessed the girl wasn't much older than he was, but it was hard to tell. She wore no shoes or jewelry. Oliver looked quite genteel by comparison.

But what was most peculiar to Oliver was the girl's face. At first, Oliver thought it was dirty, or she'd gotten into some blackberry pie that stained her face a light shade of purple-pink. Nor was it neat, rather, it looked like it was applied forcefully, with an unkind hand — something Oliver knew all too well. But most of all, Oliver recognized the face of someone who hadn't eaten. "What happened to you?"

The look she gave said she had the same question about Oliver. But now was not the time for explanations. Heavy footfalls snapped sticks somewhere to his right. Sticking his head out, Oliver made out a man in the distance and the glint of a gun.

He was joined a moment later by a woman dressed in a dark, long-coat. She held a narrow tube in one hand. They had the look of ruffians about them, a look he'd seen in every dark alley in London. As they searched the forest, Oliver cowered.

"Be careful of the darts. Best to dodge them. They'll make you ill, they will," the girl said. "Come this way, and quietly, if you want to stay safe."

Oliver did as he was told, creeping behind the girl as softly as his feet would allow. They went up the hill, toward the river and back where she first ran into him. He briefly wondered if he should leave her and find the watch, but the girl grabbed his sleeve and dragged him along, while the footfalls behind him grew louder.

The river was close, he could hear it. Only this time, the water sounded differently. Louder, and more alive. It covered the noise they made, but it also drowned out the sounds around them. He risked speaking to her once more.

"Where are we going?"

"Toward the water, and any airship moored there. Toward life away from here." A quizzical expression perched on her face. "How'd you make it out here so long? Unless you're one of the Lords? You have such a look about you—"

"Airship?"

"Of course."

"Are we safe?" Oliver asked.

"For a moment. We might've lost them. But best to be careful. There's always Lords and Littles out by the water. Keep low and close."

Oliver hung on every word. This was a strange land, far stranger than the streets of London, but not altogether unrecognizable in some horrible, familiar ways. He was about to ask for the girl's name, for he had questions of his own, when they went around an outcropping and found themselves face-to-face with a stout fellow. He eyed them greedily. "You two aren't in your proper places."

The man shot out his fist and Oliver stumbled back, dizzy and confused against the blow. He felt the bone around his eye crack and his face swell. Light flashed and a blaze of pain overwhelmed him before the world started going dark, and as it did, the girl cried out.

***

Oliver awoke on his own to a feeling of being utterly lost. He'd been alone before, on his long walk to London. But there, he'd nearly died. Now, he was without the other workhouse children, without Jack and Charley. Without the strange watch… and without the strange girl, though he didn't even know her name.

As he regained his senses, he could smell food from the next room. He got to his feet, wondering if it was him or the room itself which seemed to sway. He wandered to the door, noting that it was opened. The whole place seemed light and airy. The walls were thin, as if more paper than brick. The floor under him was a honeycomb weave of rope and string. The whole structure seemed a flower, ushering him to a circular room at the center.

In the room, he came across a rounded wooden table, set for two. At one end sat the strange fellow who'd hit him. Oliver gently touched his eye and found that it was sore and swollen.

"There, there, all is well!" the man said. He boasted a round belly and expensive garb of silk, embroidered with all manner and color of gems. His skin was an unnatural shade that clashed with an ill-fitting mop of reddish brown hair. "Had to sort things out earlier, apologies abound, but best to let those in charge put things to rights. No need to put up a fight when what needs doing gets done, as I say, and you looked like you might resist, though you don't have the look of a delinquent, do you? A mystery you are, my Little-lord! A straight enigma."

Everything the man said came out at an exclamation, an octave or four above where it should, as if he were a costermonger hawking his wares. Oliver had grown used to noise and it didn't bother him as much as it should. In fact, the man's boisterous nature seemed to license Oliver to speak freely.

"Where is the girl who was with me?" Being bold had gotten him in trouble before. But he had to know. "Is she alright? I heard her scream."

"The girl?" the man started. "She's fine, though doing better than she should, I suppose. And as to her whereabouts, well, seeing as how you're standing at the top of the tower, then you must reason that she is below! Straight at the bottom, that one, with her kind, as it should be," the man said. "Come, you must be starving and food we have. Have the chair opposite mine. Nell is fine."

Nell was the name then. He was glad to know it, and even gladder to know she was safe, or so he was told. Oliver pulled out a chair and sat in silence, wondering what his next move should be, what his next question should be, or if he should say anything at all. The man hadn't said or done anything yet to set Oliver at ease.

A moment later, a boy, his face dyed like Nell's, entered with a small bowl that gave off a wispy aroma of broth. Oliver sat straight, his tongue already tasting it before it was ladled into the bowl. Once it was, he slurped it down greedily.

The man laughed. "Oh, I knew the Little-lord was hungry. I have a knack for these things, knowing stuff as I do. Toad they call me, but unless you're a fly, I won't bite, not nearly as quick as you swallowed that bowl, I might add."

Oliver stopped. His bowl was empty, though his tummy wished it weren't. The man seemed jovial enough. Perhaps it wouldn't hurt… no, he'd gone plenty of times with less. He'd be fine. Which is why he surprised himself when, "I want some more," slipped through his lips.

The man laughed even louder. "Oh, you don't know, do you? Perhaps you are a delinquent after all. We'll get to the bottom of it, sure enough, but tongues talk easier when little tummies are tuckered, eh?" He laughed again, wiping away a bead of broth dripping down his chin. "My dear boy, this is just the beginning. Bring out the rest of the courses," he hollered excitedly into the other room.

Soon, Oliver's plate was loaded with fresh capons, salted snails, pippin pies, and roasted duck. It was more food all in one spot than Oliver had seen altogether in his lifetime. And they were bringing out pastries and bread still!

His nose wagged with the wafting air of baked pears, cooked sausages, and poached eggs which warmed and filled him at the same time. But that didn't stop him from tearing into a duck and guzzling down a sweet, thick red wine. Oliver felt full and happy for the first time in his life.

As Oliver stuffed a scone into his mouth, Toad caught his attention with a clink of a spoon to his glass. "Now then, Little-lord, set things to right. Bring us to law and order, right and wrong. Start with a name perhaps? You have an awfully pleasant countenance that I can't place. I must know everything."

Oliver swallowed a scratchy bit of the scone, realizing at once what the man was after. He didn't know, aside from his name, anything he could tell the man that would satisfy his questions; not when Oliver had so many of his own.

He certainly didn't want the man knowing his name, because that was the only real thing left. But he couldn't lie, could he? Was it really so far a distance to walk from thievery to lying, all in one day?

Toad banged the spoon once more. "You got two options here: talk or starve. This'll be your only meal from now on." He tossed an end of bread Oliver's way. "You answer, and maybe, just maybe, your place will be up here with me instead of down below with your friend Nell, who you'll have to fight with for crumbs."

Oliver pushed the plate away, frowning. Toad's outburst reminded him of London, of all the men who appeared gentle, only to be stern with the switch. He wanted to throw up all of Toad's food he'd eaten and the way his stomach lurched he wasn't sure he'd be able to keep it down anyway.

"Well?"

"Tom," Oliver said, the lie churning away in his tummy. It was the first name he could think of. "Tom White." It was a common enough name, he supposed, a name he'd heard Bobbies use when they didn't know a man's name. It was a plain name, but it wasn't the truth. He'd never lied before. And it hurt.

"Well, Tom! That wasn't so bad. A good thing to say one's name, innit? And so, where does young Tom White come from?"

"Greenland, sir." The next lie was easier. Quicker too. He didn't know what a Greenland was, but the forest and the trees and the leaves he'd found himself in earlier gave the statement a touch of truth.

Toad appeared puzzled, as if there was an answer to this riddle, but it was locked far away in the back of his brain. "Greenland, you say?"

he said with a snort. "Sooner you swam from Atlantis, I'd gather! How'd you manage the travel then? How'd you slip off the airship?"

"I didn't take an airship. I walked." Everywhere Oliver went, he'd walked. At least that answer was the truth.

Toad snortled. "A clever, funny lad. I'll grant you the joke, but only because it humors me. Let's keep it at that." He grew serious once more. "I don't recall a place called Greenland, except in ancient talk. Covered in ice, it was, and not at all a proper name for a place as mystical as that. Imagine, water as ice!"

Toad laughed again, but this time at himself. "Not many places built upwards as we did. Not many people could. Still, there could be a settlement of sorts now in that area. It would explain your odd look. Come, I'll ask again, by what means did you travel here?"

Oliver couldn't well explain the watch, the odd man with the hat, and things beyond his understanding, not least because he didn't have the watch anymore as proof. And even if he did, he didn't trust Toad with it. Maybe Toad would try to use it to go back. London already had plenty of people like him. It didn't need another.

He needed to decide. He could make up a story, hopefully convince Toad of its truth and maybe live out his life high in the tower, with plenty of food to eat. Good food. Delicious beyond anything he could fathom. Part of him desired it. He could not deny it. But what was it the man with the hat told him? *Keep to your innocence.* Nell was down there somewhere, along with many others, he was sure of it. As strange as this place was, it reeked under the surface with the same smells as London.

"To be honest, sir, when I got here, I became a little thrown. Nell found me. I'm sure she could help put this together. Might we go down there and check on her?"

After a long pause, Toad answered with a rub of his chin. "I suppose so, we can go down now. Sort this whole thing out. But mind you, if you're a delinquent like the lot of 'em, I got my dye ready for you, I do. We must have law!"

Oliver grabbed a roll, and then another, and tucked them along with two pink pastries inside a napkin.

"Are you thinking to give those to your friend? I assure you she won't need them. I provide for them all, as much as they deserve, even moreso if you ask others. I'm a man of charity, you know. Put them back, Tom. I'll have the table cleared and the food dumped while we are gone."

Oliver put the food back, hoping he didn't just hear Toad say that all this food would be thrown out as rubbish. He groaned inwardly as he followed Toad out the room and into a contraption that looked to him like an oversized basket. He felt light as the two were lowered to the ground. The tops of trees came into view and he traced branches downward as they descended, not realizing just how high up they were.

On the ground, at the base of the tower, was a large complex dug partway into the earth, with skeletal iron fingers serving as both the base of Toad's tower and a prison to those inside. Oliver's heart fell when he spotted Nell among the crowd of purple-faced people. It was the workhouse all over again.

She been beaten. A gash above her eye trailed her cheek, dripping down off her face and soaking through her garb. Her other eye was blackened, like Oliver's. Her left arm was full of bruises, as if she were dragged the whole way here. He ran up to the bars to her.

"See? She's no worse for wear, as I said. I am straight if nothing else, else a crooked man I'd be."

"How about if we called you a crooked toad, then?" A man and a woman stepped out of the forest and onto the clearing, then strutted over to the tower. Oliver recognized them as the pair that chased after Nell. They both still wore long-coats, despite the heat. The woman carried a long, thin pipe, but the man's gun was missing.

"That girl," the man said, "She belongs to us."

"Good to see you again, Billy, but technically, she belongs to me," Toad croaked, "She's a nasty one, she is. Slipped through my fingers again, but by and large, mine. She won't escape again."

"Ah, but she escaped nonetheless. We found her out in the woods; that makes her a bounty. No fair you pilfering what was ours to return. You get paid plenty by the Powers for housing these delinquents, keeping them off the streets, maintaining that law you're always preachin' on about. You trying to push us down with the Purple People too? These delinquents? Trying to cut us out? That's not right."

"I can see you're feeling a might sensitive over the matter." Toad looked a bit nervous, as if out of his element when not in the air. "I had business by the docks and stumbled across them, took matters into my own hands is all, I meant no foul." He pointed to Nell and Oliver.

The pair took note. "Who's the boy? He worth any silver?"

Oliver cringed at that.

"I was in the midst of piecing it out. I'll have some pieces for you if we can just take this up to the tower and talk it over like the highborn we are."

"I don't think so. Not this time." The man moved aside the long flap of his coat and brought out the gun. Oliver froze in fright.

Toad, in contrast, laughed. "Last time you pulled that thing out on me, you didn't even have a slice of silver for a bullet. We all had a laugh. But I'm in no humor today. Put that empty thing away. It won't work on me."

"Oh, I've got one, bless me. Bullet over food. And now we're starving and we're aiming to take what you've got. Give us the boy and what you stole from us for taking the girl. Then we'll have it back to rights."

"Or would you rather I stick you with a sick dart?" The woman said. "Take you weeks to recover and when you do, we'll send you far away from here. Maybe you'll be a delinquent in someone else's tower, while we settle into yours. If we take everything, you won't have the means to take it back."

"It's kinda hard to prove you're a Lord with that purple stuff dyed all over your face," Billy said widening his stance. "It's been a long time coming for you."

Toad's faced reddened. He crept toward the safety of the basket. As he kept his guard toward his attackers, he left himself vulnerable from behind, where Oliver stood.

"Keys," Nell whispered, pointing to Toad's pocket.

Oliver nodded in understanding. He waited for his chance, and as Billy moved forward, Oliver slipped the keys out silently.

"I'll raise your rates, I promise you. Maybe throw in a good word with the other tower owners. Just don't take what's mine."

Billy eyed the boy. "He doesn't look like he's from around here. I think he's worth something. Could be gold to a guy like me. So, I'll offer a trade. I'll give you a bullet in the heart and I'll take the kid."

"No." Toad made for the basket, reaching the edge and nearly falling in. Once inside, he called out, "Pull up, pull up with all haste!" Slowly, the basket lifted off the ground.

The woman took the tube and blew a dart at Toad, but it lodged harmlessly into the wicker weaving. That left a lone bullet from Billy. In that still moment of indecision as Toad made his escape climbing higher in the sky, Oliver tossed the keys to Nell.

An instant later, the iron gates flew open with a crash and the prisoners poured out.

"You took my keys! After my kindness? You filthy brat, I'll have you," Toad screamed down at him. He yelled at the purple-faced prisoner hoisting him up. "Let me down, let me down!"

It was the wrong thing to say. The purple-faced man shot Toad a sly smile. And, at a height of just above the trees, he let go of the rope.

The basket plummeted. Toad's scream stopped suddenly with a sickening squelch.

Nell took Oliver's hand. "This way! Back to the water."

The rest of the delinquents seemed to be heading the same way. Oliver followed, asking, "Why are we leaving? Toad is gone!"

"There are plenty more people like him behind us. Someone else will take his post if those two hunters don't manage it themselves. The woman blew sick darts at the fleeing prisoners.

At that, Oliver made off in a sprint, just as he did when called a thief earlier… today, was it? Nell was right there beside him, keeping up despite her injuries. She smiled at him, as if in thanks. "We get to the airships, get one going, we'll be alright. There's land beyond the seas here, and they'll have to take us in. They'll have to rescue us from all this. I know they will."

Oliver wasn't so sure, but he plowed ahead anyway at full steam. If she wanted to escape, he'd do his best to see her safe. It was the least he could do, to help her leave a world that wasn't too different from his own. And it was time for him to go home too if only he could find that watch again.

It wasn't that far to the river. Of course, once they got there, Oliver realized the body of water in front of him wasn't a river at all. Instead, it was a deep-blue expanse, farther than his eyes could see. It had to be the ocean, though he'd never seen it. Of course, Oliver couldn't fathom there ever being this much water all at one spot. After everything he'd seen today, the sight was still unbelievable.

"It covers almost everything. Has for ages," she said without waiting for a question. "You really aren't from around here. You haven't even looked up to see the ships."

When Oliver saw them, he let out a gasp. Towers encircled the beach and moored to them were flying wooden ships. Above each ship was, what looked to Oliver, an enormous grey pillowcase, lumpy, but also somehow light and full of air. It was if a ship turned its sails into a mishappen ball and sailed skyward, like a kite. Around the stern of each ship, a long iron nozzle jutted out. It didn't look like any cannon he'd seen before.

The others were running down to the beach; some were already crawling up towers. What Lords there were scattered at the sight of so many Littles. Nell and her people were free. He smiled. It would all work out.

He felt a prick on his neck. She cried to him, her voice stretched and scratched with alarm. "You've been hit!"

Oliver grabbed at his neck and found a small needle in his hand as Nell pulled Oliver down into cover. Several prisoners took notice and started heading back their way.

"What is this?"

"It's a means to keep control," she answered. "You get stuck, and within minutes, you get sick. You need weeks to mend. It's costly. And then you're theirs, marked with this," she finished, pointing to her face.

"I'm fine. I don't feel a thing."

Nell forced out a laugh. "There's strength in you, I can tell. But everyone needs help at some time. I won't let them take you."

"It doesn't matter. I have to get my watch. If I can get to it, I can escape."

"You're not coming with us?"

Oliver hadn't really considered going with her until she mentioned it. He thought about it. The idea of running away was appealing. "I can't." He'd already left London. And things weren't much better here. Maybe running away wasn't the answer.

His neck was already starting to stiffen. "You go on ahead. I'm close to the watch. I can hear it, the ticking, though don't know how. I'll grab it and meet you on the ship and see you safe before I leave, I promise."

"I'm going with you," she smiled. "Someone's got to keep you safe first." She talked to the others, "Go, ready the ship and take off, we're heading back in the woods."

Oliver didn't think he could argue with her, so rubbing his neck, he plunged back in among the trees.

***

The path before him darkened under the canopy. She followed him as he listened for the watch, the ticking growing louder as he neared. A bit further on, Oliver thought he spotted the broken branches of the bush he and Nell landed in earlier. The ticking stopped. Oliver strained to listen, but instead of hearing the watch, he heard something else.

He knew it was Billy and the woman. They'd been close enough to shoot him, though he guessed that had been mostly dumb luck. But, as Oliver slowed and examined his surroundings, he spotted the couple a stone's throw away.

Oliver and Nell ducked down in the undergrowth, bramble branches once again slicing through his cloths and scratching him. They crept as quickly as they dared, away from the hunters. A minute later, as he reached the spot where he thought the watch was, Oliver lost sight of them.

He was about to breathe again, when there was a single, loud crack of thunder.

Oliver's heart skipped, and a prickly feeling ran under his skin from head to toe. He'd never heard a sound as vile and violent before. His ears rang, and his head throbbed, but as it subsided, he heard the woman saying something.

"…you wasted the bullet."

"Eh, after this, we'll have all the bullets we need. Besides, we don't need the girl, Toad's right, she's always escaping. We don't want to be paying hunters of our own, eh? We just need the boy."

The girl? Oliver search around, unable to breath. She was nowhere to be seen. He raced back to where he'd last seen her standing, only to see her laying in the dirt, a red, round circle expanding across her chest. She looked sickly and pale, sweat beading across her forehead, air gasping between her lips.

"No, no!" Oliver shook violently. Nell couldn't die. He'd stay, he'd stay here forever if it meant she would live. Surely, she could live?

"I'm fine, I don't feel a thing," Nell mocked, as the pain in her breath and face betrayed every word. "Do you ever feel like your life only gets in the way of everyone else?" she asked. "Like your life… doesn't matter?"

Oliver nodded.

"I don't. I was nobody. But I stood against the wind any chance I could. Most days, I was blown over," Nell coughed up a bit of blood.

"But sometimes… I flew." She pointed a weak hand skyward. Oliver saw a shadow forming over the trees.

"What are we going to do now?" The woman asked Billy.

"Take the boy, see how much he's worth to the right person. A stranger like that ought to fetch a price. He's got to have some useful bit of news that will fetch a fine nugget. Could be he's from a land not swallowed over."

At that, a tree crashed down as several bursts of gunfire cut through from the airship overhead. Branches cracked, splinters flew, and dirt exploded into the air, sending the couple diving away. The fallen tree settled down, blocking the couples' path. When the two tried to rise, gunfire erupted again from the airship, sending Billy and the woman running off into the woods.

A moment later, a basket was lowered from the airship and an older man came over and knelt next to Nell. He looked over the situation, took her wrist, and shook his head slowly. "I'm sorry, she will pass on from this world."

Tears stung Oliver's eyes. "Isn't there anything we can do?"

The man shook his head again. "We need to go, before others like them come back."

"I can't. I can't leave her."

"It's all right," Nell said. "I'll be at peace soon. My life will have meant something." She said weakly, "Do you see the trees? Aren't they beautiful?"

Yes, of course Oliver could see the trees. They were all around him. What did that have to do with anything?

"A long time ago, everything you see here was rubbish, fields of trash. These hills were made from mounds of garbage. Heaps upon heaps of it, piled higher to escape the rising waters. It was the very refuse people threw away, discarded at whim," Nell coughed more. There was blood rushing out everywhere soaking Oliver's hands. She continued, through several last shallow breathes, "But look at the trees. Look at what grew. There is beauty here." She smiled. "Even when our roots grow in waste… we can still rise tall…"

"No!" Oliver cradled her head, placing it on his lap. As he did so, he saw his watch. As he took it, he thought of the man with the tall hat back in London, the one who'd given him the watch. If the man had a watch that could do all this, what else did he have?

"He can save her, I know he can!" Oliver said with some measure of determination. "But I have to go. I have to take her with me."

The man shook his head. "She is beyond saving. Do what you must. And thank you for your part in freeing us."

"Where will you go?"

He pointed to the airship. "Where the wind takes us. Where there is a better land for us to live. There must be a place beyond the seas."

"I hope you find it."

With that, the man stepped into the basket, and the airship cast off. In the distance, more hunters were shouting. And the shouts grew closer.

Oliver recovered the timepiece from its place on the forest floor by Nell's hand. He twisted the crown backwards, counting the times it turned, hoping he got it right. Was it twelve spins or thirteen? He couldn't remember. A group of Lords were approaching, weapons drawn. He grabbed on tightly to Nell and flipped the pocket watch open as guns burst.

***

The smell of the Thames hit him before the water did. He landed on the muddy bank, she landed afloat in the mucky river. He tried to hold on, but the quick current carried her out of his arms.

"No!" But it was too late. She was already gone. Tears dropped into the river, lost to the water. "I was going to save her…"

He'd lost her.

He remembered what she'd said about the trees, about life, about how cruel it was. Lords across time argued against each other, and as they did, as problems went unsolved, it was the little ones like Oliver who suffered. As he'd seen for himself, that hadn't changed in the future either.

Not unless he could stop it. He wouldn't let that happen and the best way to do that, he knew, was to make the most out of the present. From that moment, he'd endure whatever tortures awaited him. If he survived, he'd change things. He knew he could. But if he didn't make it, and he knew he might not, he'd live so that his story would serve as Nell's had, as an inspiration to others.

The clanging of the church bells began, reminding Oliver of what he still needed to do. Wiping away tears, he said goodbye to her as she floated away, beyond his reach and his control.

The watch no longer pulled him. He limped down the street, each passing step more difficult than the last. He put a hand to his neck, feeling the prick of the dart. The drug had started to take effect.

He stopped at the corner where he'd left earlier and spotted a strange sight. It was… *him*. And he was listening to the man with the hat. It shook him for a moment, and he nearly yelled out, especially when the other Oliver disappeared a moment later. He thought he understood, near as he could, that it was the old Oliver that vanished, starting the journey he'd just finished. And here he was. Back already.

Down the hill, the crowd of people who were chasing him earlier spotted him. He could hear screams of, "There he is!" The crowd started after him again.

The man with the black hat and red quill gestured to Oliver and then turned down a small alleyway. Oliver followed.

"I'd say thank you for bringing me my watch, but, to me, you never left." The man winked, "although it's been a bit longer for you, I imagine."

"What was that all about? If you knew what was going to happen, how could you do that to Nell?"

The man ignored Oliver and instead stepped into small shop. From a few steps back, Oliver could see knick-knacks of all sorts through the window. From its wares, it looked to him like a curiosity shop. He peered in through the semi-opened door to see Nell laying on top of a counter inside. Oliver's heart nearly leapt out of his mouth.

"She's out of time."

Oliver, frowned, but before he could well a tear, the odd man's smile stopped him.

"No, no, that's not what I meant. I assure you, she is fine. I meant… well what I meant is harder to explain. I promise you she's on the mend."

"How?"

"How, asks the boy who just traveled through time?" The man's cheeks lit up, "trust me, dear boy, there are things that may seem extraordinary to you, but are quite routine for me."

Oliver was confused. And the sickness dragging at him wasn't helping. The man seemed to sense his unease as he continued, "Be assured that she is well. There's another story in her yet."

The man was more a mystery than he could imagine, but that didn't matter. He'd saved Nell. So far, he was the most decent person Oliver had met.

"I wish I could take you on, Oliver," the man said. "You'd make a fine companion, but the dickens would have me if I did. I've meddled enough." He took his watch and his leave, but not before nodding once more as he said, "Besides, your story is here, where you have much still to tell. Remember, your course will foreshadow certain ends if continued, but if the course has changed," he said, rather cryptically, holding out the pocket watch, "so will the end." At that, the man shut the door and Oliver was alone in the alley.

He wasn't quite sure he understood all that, but he knew the words would stick with him, so he had plenty of time to work them out, but not before the crowd of people were on him, surrounding him on both sides of the thin alley. The dart had him now. He was slumping over with sickness. It overcame him, and the words and experiences of the last day muddled together. He hardly felt the flash of pain when a burly man smashed a hairy hand into Oliver's face.

But as the blackness took him, Oliver smiled. He'd wake up again, and when he did, he knew just where to find Nell.

End.

Notes for A Twist in Time

It's probably a bit naïve of me to presume I could pluck a classic Dickens' character out of his world for my own sinister purposes, so it's probably even more presumptuous that this short story inspired me to write a screenplay and several novels. I've now created my own world inhabited by Dickens' great characters. I mean, if you're going to steal, steal from the best and go all in, right?

This original short story was inspired by Seth Grahame-Smith's spunky *Pride and Prejudice and Zombies*. I loved how he wove his own femme-fatale tale around Austen's classic romance and brought it to a new, rabid audience. I wanted to do the same with the themes present in Dickens' works by presenting them in a fun way to new readers.

This story was first published by Inklings Press in *Tales of Wonder*. You can read further adventures of Oliver Twist in my novel series *A Twist in Time*.

Lost Treasure

Lucy Sharvet knew they weren't going to like what she'd painted. Again.

The seven-year-old clutched a canvas close to her chest, careful not to smear paint on her new superhero t-shirt. Hidden away from those prying eyes was her art project. She loved art. It was her favorite subject. And she wanted nothing more than to paint all the time. But no one liked her pictures, least of all her classmates.

On their desks were paintings of puppies, rainbows, magical forests full of fairies, a pirate ship full of treasure, and one wicked looking dinosaur. A T-Rex, Lucy believed, though the arms weren't as stunted as they were supposed to be, and it had too many claws. And they'd forgotten feathers.

Yet, despite his many mistakes, when Rude Ricardo showed it to the class, everyone had gasped in excitement. Even though he always teased her, she still liked his painting. Very much. The same was true of Petrie's pirates and Lakesha's forest.

I can't show them mine. Everyone will laugh at me. They'll say it was stupid and Rude Ricardo will call me Lucy-Goosey again.

"Lucille," her scary old teacher called her. Lucy hated being called that. No one called her Lucille. Except for Ms Clark, with her skin so tight on her face it looked like she had a skull for a head, like the one on the black flag in Petrie's painting. "Show us your work."

Lucy did what she was told, because what else was she supposed to do? Slowly, she turned her painting around. Sure enough, laughter erupted in the classroom. Petrie pointed at her. Lakesha's laugh was like a continuous squeak across a white board. And of course, Rude Ricardo had his say: "Lucy-Goosey, Lucy-Goosey, she's so goofy!"

She couldn't stop the tears from coming. She tried, she really had tried, but they came all the same.

Lucy had painted a picture of a white house, outlined in red, with a red-tiled roof and red window frames and a nice green garden and a tall tree in the yard with a tire swing hanging off a branch and it was perfect...

"Lucille," Ms Clark called. "Turn your picture right-side up."

Lucy shook her head. *I knew everyone would laugh. I knew they would think I had held out my painting wrong.* She told her class, "It's not upside down."

Pointing to the bottom, across from the roof, was her name. It was scribbled in black, the letters all going the right way.

She hadn't flipped the painting by accident. She hadn't turned it upside down at all. In fact, she had gone so far as to paint everything the way it appeared, starting with the roof on the bottom and working her way up, rather than taking the cheat.

It's how her painting had appeared in her mind. It's how her brushes and paint had spoken to her. It's what she had wanted to do. Like everyone else had, from Ricardo's cool dinosaur to Lakesha's amazing fairy forest. So why did they laugh at *her?*

"Ms Lucille Sharvet—" her teacher began. But before she finished, the bell interrupted. It rang out like an angel singing. Her pain was over, for the moment. Lucy wiped away tears and sniffled and felt her skin cool. The embarrassment ended as everyone ignored her to hurriedly shove school supplies into their backpacks. Shouldering them, they all started for the exit door. Lucy placed her painting carefully on her desk and did the same.

"Okay, class," Ms Clark caught the fleeing class' attention by standing in front of the door, keeping it closed. "Tomorrow is career day. Paint a picture of who you want to be." She turned her eerie gaze to Lucy but spoke loud enough so that everyone could hear over the din: "And be sure to know which way is up."

Lucy's tears fell down her cheeks all during her slow walk home.

***

Later, when her tears had dried, Lucy gave thought to tomorrow's Career Day. She had no idea what she wanted to be when she grew up. She had thought to maybe be an artist …or something else. An archeologist, perhaps. Digging around in the dirt, uncovering something new and exciting like a buried treasure or a new dinosaur bone.

Or maybe she would work with animals, like the nice lady at the zoo she saw working with the snakes. Lucy had even held one, a soft rosy-pink snake that tickled her arm as it slithered up to boop her nose with its tongue. She had liked that. Though she was still afraid of them. The nice lady at the zoo had made her feel brave. Maybe Lucy could do work with animals too.

But being all grown up seemed super-far distant. It was as far away to Lucy as her home was to the moon. Tonight, though, there was no moon at all. The sky was dark, with grey scary clouds and flashes of lightning and the rumbling of thunder around her. Bones seemed so boring and old, and animals seemed scary and dangerous.

Even if she could decide on who she might be and did paint herself as a tall, big person wearing a jungle hat, her class would just laugh at her again. Ms Clark would poke fun. Ricardo would be rude. Why do the homework at all? Why even go to school in the morning? Maybe she could be sick.

By the time she was called down to dinner, her canvas was still blank. She stirred her stew all through the meal, though she was hungry enough to eat the whole pot. "How was school today, Little Lucy?" Her daddy asked her.

"It was okay," she said, keeping silent through the rest of the meal and excusing herself, her potatoes and carrots and roast beef all uneaten. And she kept to herself all evening, the bare canvas by her side, even as her daddy tucked her in and tried to persuade her to eat some apple slices and then, on giving up, he read to her from *Harry Potter*. He always did the voices wrong.

Yet, his reading usually sent her to sleep.

Long after he had kissed her goodnight and left her alone with nothing but her nightlight and her thoughts, she lay in bed, with absolutely no idea what to paint for tomorrow's class. And even if she did figure something out, everyone, she was sure, would tease her.

She had been thinking about drawing a picture of herself as an artist, despite her classmates' laughter, when the crazy thing happened. She'd pictured an image of her with longer hair kept down, standing much taller and wearing a smock, next to an easel, holding a brush. But the idea vanished as her bedroom began to shimmer.

Bedrooms don't shimmer, do they?

It had never happened before. And she didn't recall anyone else ever mentioning the odd movements of their walls, or the tiny shivers crawling through their skin. She'd only seen stuff like that in movies or on her tablet. *That was all pretend, wasn't it?*

At first, a rippling came across her walls. When her room rippled again, Lucy had the sense of being underwater as waves washed over her. Her tummy rolled with each rocking motion, just like it did when her daddy took her on drives through winding mountain roads.

Just when she didn't think she could take it anymore, just before she began to lean over her bed to hurl, the wave-like motion stilled. If that had been all, Lucy would have stayed sitting-up in her bed. She would have chalked it up to being hungry, then she would have lain back down and gone to sleep, her canvas untouched.

Instead, a burst of blackness – a darker black than she had ever seen, even in all the paints from all the stores – tore a hole out of the center of her room, beyond the foot of her bed. The hole widened; blue-purple tendrils of lightning snaked out. Hairs on Lucy's arms raised.

She should have been scared. She should have covered herself with her blankets and shivered with fear, or dove under her bed and cried, or dashed out the door and into her daddy's arms. Lucy scooted across her bed, closer to the dark void. A hand emerged. A foot. Followed by a leg. Then a torso. Soon, a strange man in his entirety appeared.

She gulped as the stranger stood in front of her. The man, she thought, seemed confused. He cast his eyes about her room like he was searching for something. Something that wasn't there.

He was dressed in what looked like a deep, blue-colored wetsuit. But the chest, elbows, and knees were patched in some sort of tightly interwoven yellow and black threads. His hair was blonde and dark stubble poked through his chin, though even with the dull nightlight on the desk behind him, Lucy could not see his eyes clearly.

Her focus went from his face to his hands. He carried some sort of strange computer. Or was it a phone, maybe? It was larger and thicker than one, but smaller than her tablet. A blue screen came on, illuminating dirty, rough hands that waved the contraption slowly across the room, throwing shadows across the walls.

"Who-o," she started, working up the courage to address the stranger. She hadn't quite decided if she should scream. Her daddy would know what to do. Still, the man looked lost. And didn't her daddy say that people should help other people? "Who are you?"

The man gave a grunt after circling the room hurriedly. He half-whispered, half growled, "Who are you?"

"I'm Lucy." She decided to put on a brave face and at least be polite. When she said her name, the man stopped looking around the room. He stared at her.

"Lucille Sharvet?"

"Don't call me that. I hate that name. My daddy calls me his Little Lucy."

"Well," he said, with a sigh of relief. "I'm in the right place …but the wrong time." He scratched at his chin. "What grade are you in?"

"Second."

He nodded in response, as if he'd just been called to do a math problem on the white board in front of the class. Lucy hated numbers. Just as much as cooked carrots. "Hmmm, Little Second-Grader-Lucy, it looks like I'm about," he gestured on his fingers like he was counting, like she had to do, "Well, the nav-computer's input date is correct." The date of October 24th, 2040 appeared on the screen. *That's today,*

Lucy thought, *but nowhere near the year*. The man finished. "The current must have taken me back about two decades too soon."

He slapped the side of the device.

"Too soon for what?"

"Look kid, being in a lass's room in the middle of the night, as you might surmise, is understandably awkward. I've got to get back to my ship." He began to play with the blue screen, moving away from the bed.

"A ship?"

He didn't respond. Sometimes, when daddy was busy, he wouldn't respond either. She just had to speak louder. "Are you an alien?" But he didn't look like a creature from another planet. He looked human, unshaven, what she could see of his hair looked messy, and he wore some sort of clothing suited for the water. Who else traveled in ships and was grungy and dirty? "Are you a pirate?"

The man spun around, a finger to his lips, shushing her.

That was so like Ms Clark.

"Whisper, would you?"

"Tell me and I will. Otherwise, I'll get my daddy. I shouldn't have strangers in my room, even if you do look lost."

He put his hands out, urging her to stop. She did.

"As a matter of fact, I am a pirate."

Lucy sat at the foot of the bed, the man silhouetted by her window and framed by Starry Night curtains. "But you can't be. Where's your eyepatch?"

"I have an iPad instead." He held out the machine in his hand. Then lowered it as if in shame. "Sorry, stupid joke. It's a chronometer. It kinda looks like the iPads of your age, though, right?"

Lucy didn't know what a chronometer was, but she doubted she could say the word back, so she ignored the strange comment and looked at the pirate's feet.

"Where's your peg leg?"

"These are still good." He moved his hands to his sides and patted his legs, shaking his head. "Listen, I've got to go—"

"Where's your bird?"

"Ahh, now you're talking." He slowed, maybe unsure if he should keep going. But she wanted to know. A real live pirate, in her room, and he had a bird! "Now a few of those I've got. Rare and priceless ones. A Mauritian dodo from the Ice Age. A dozen caged Lord Howe gerygones. And most prized of all, a live *Archaeopteryx*."

That word, Lucy *did* know. And she could even say it. It was a hundred-and-fifty-million-year-old creature that had once lived with dinosaurs and had since died out. Gone ex-stinked, her daddy had said.

Having one, a real live one, was amazing. Her eyes opened widely, but the more she thought on it, the quicker they closed into squints. "That's not possible."

"I figured you'd like that one. Though it's probably a bit much to understand. You see, I'm a time pirate."

"A what?"

"I really shouldn't say," The pirate said. "But I can see you're a bright lass. I like you."

"Tell me everything." *It all sounds so exciting.*

His eyes went wide and bright as he explained, "My ship and crew navigate the time-currents, the different timelines between Earths." He shook his head, then began again, holding the chrono-something back up. "I can cross the multiverse, pluck rare items from different Earths, then, my crew sells them elsewhere for a share of the plunder. Time pirates."

"Is that why you are here? How did you know my name? My real name? The one I hate?"

"Clever girl," he said, rubbing his chin. "I'm not telling you that one. Just so you don't know too much. I'll try and explain else-wise. I really don't meet many others who share my excitement, who even believe me." Lucy offered him an apple slice, which he accepted with a smile and slid in his mouth. "But then I must be on my way – deal?"

Lucy spat on her hand and held it out. The pirate hesitated, then took an edge of her finger with the tips of his own, mindful of the spit, and shook.

"We steal from a timeline, for example, where history was different. An Earth where Shakespeare wrote an 11th tragedy. Or from an Earth where the Beatles never broke up. Or perhaps a timeline on an Earth where people have never read Bertie Wells' novel, *The Chronic Argonauts,* one of my favorites. Kept a first edition for myself."

"Who?"

"Precisely." He smiled, thinly. "Those timelines then go on, none the wiser, never knowing what was lost. A perfect theft."

Waving a hand in the air, the man bowed. She'd seen a few villains on TV, proud of the naughty things they'd done, behave in such a way. Perhaps he was a pirate after all.

"And then in other timelines, on Earths hungry for such lost artifacts, a discerning collector might want their own private but *very* authentic copy of such an artifact, like say, of an album of Elvis music or a …particular painting," he said, eyeing her. She couldn't make out their color; she desperately wished to see his whole face. "Well, that's treasure in my chest."

Finished, he gave no indication of an encore flourish. Instead, the pirate breathed out as if relieved and brought his blue screen up in front of him again, ignoring her. *But there are so many more questions I have.*

Her walls pulsed again and suddenly she felt deep underwater once more. Everything from her dresser to her curtains to her bed shimmered as waves of… energy? She didn't know what it was. She only knew that she had so much more to learn before the mysterious man disappeared.

"Why did you look so lost when you arrived?" It wasn't the best question she could have asked. But it was the first one on her mind and she had blurted it out.

"Look, kid, you can get caught in a time-current, like a riptide. You end up in The Bahamas instead of the Carolinas, get my drift? The computer brought me to you, but the tides and currents swept me back too far." The black void, darker and blacker than the deepest part of night reappeared. Before the pirate stepped through, he told her, "I'll see you and your masterpiece in a second. Well, longer for you, of course…”

What did the pirate mean by that? And why had he come to her room? *Am I dreaming?*

And like that, the man vanished, and the room went back to normal. She didn't feel the urge to vomit anymore. It all sounded so fantastical, so incredible, like if Escher and Dali, two of her favorite artists, had conspired to paint her dreams. Her mind was alive with colors, vibrant with deep blues and bright yellows and the blackest of blacks tinged with purple.

An image of the pirate bubbled in the back of her brain. What had his screen read? He had been counting on his fingers. Was she meant to have seen that, or a carless accident on his part?

October 24, 2040. Was he coming back again that night?

Something on the floor of her room, by the wall where the pirate had disappeared through, caught her eye: something that had not been there before. She scooted closer to it and scooped it up. It was circular. Black on one side and white on the other. On the light side, there were markings that she didn't recognize. It looked like a clock, or a dial. It had only one hand and stayed still, to the left of the marks.

She didn't know what it was. But she did know that it wasn't hers. It had to have come from the pirate. *He's real. It really happened*, she smiled to herself.

A knock on the door broke her away from her thoughts.

Lucy tucked away the dial under her pillow before her daddy came in. Her skin went all prickly the way it did when she got caught doing something naughty. But she took a deep breath and tried to calm herself.

“Everything okay?” Though she could not see his face either, she pictured the way his glasses shifted on his nose whenever he was worried for her, like after she survived going down the Super Tall Slide at the fair for the first time. Once he'd calmed down, she'd gotten right back in line. “I thought I heard you talking.”

“Yeah, just thinking out loud.”

"Oh?" He stood by her bed.

"I'm going to paint something for tomorrow."

"You probably shouldn't. It's late. But if you have an idea…"

She hesitated before answering. "It's just that… I'm afraid people will laugh at me. They didn't like my painting today at school."

"Were you painting it for them, or for you?"

She shrugged. She knew the answer. She guessed that her daddy did too.

"Don't let anything stop you from you doing you," he told her. She could almost see him smile. "Let the stars be your guide, your sweat and blood and tears be your ocean …and your hard work be your wind."

"Is that from something?" Those words were pretty cool. She didn't know exactly what all of them meant, but she repeated them to herself inwardly. They found their way into her heart, etching themselves into her soul.

"I think I might have just made them up. I don't know. Probably should not have mentioned blood. Sorry."

She crawled out of bed, canvas in hand. Her daddy kissed her and left for the doorway. "Don't stay up too late, Little Lucy."

The words barely registered as she set thought to brush.

*⁎⁎

The next day, everyone in class was staring at her again, including the sunken eyes belonging to Ms Clark.

Lucy wiped away fatigue from her face and shook cobwebs from her brain. Her other classmates had already shown their paintings. Lakesha wanted to be a doctor. Petrie a teacher and Rude Ricardo had apparently wanted to be a dragon. That was, though it was painful to admit, sort of cool too.

But not as cool as mine.

"Lucille," Ms Clark caught her attention. "I hope you're not going to be an artist when you grow up?"

The whole class snickered. Rude Ricardo was the loudest. Lucy switched back to thinking he was stupid again. She shook her head.

Yes, she told herself. She loved to paint. *But no.* She may still do a painting or two, but there was something she wanted even more. Something she had to be.

She turned her painting around, revealing it – and herself – to the world. The class gasped at first, perhaps in surprise. They probably all thought she was going to pick being an artist or a zookeeper or her painting would be of her in a leather jacket in the jungle chased by a boulder. Or maybe another upside-down house.

But once they saw her painting the slow laughs started. She didn't care.

On the canvas was a large ship in the background, not unlike Petrie's pirate ship of yesterday, a jolly roger raised high with Ms Clark's face on the flag. Stars dotted the landscape among greens and blues of cresting waves. On the ship, she had painted herself, outfitted in royal blue, her short hair tied into a bun and a chrono-something in her hand.

Through a large smile, she told her class, "I'm going to be a time pirate when I grow up."

"A what?" Ms Clark burst out.

Rude Ricardo laughed so hard snot shot out his nose. Petrie turned red. Lakesha doubled over. Several of her classmates were on the floor. The whole class had lost control. She remembered when a food fight had broken out in the cafeteria, with meatballs launched like cannonballs splattering across the room. That had been tame in comparison to her classroom now.

Though tears threatened to sting her eyes, she kept them from going further. She knew she'd have to learn control, learn all sorts of things if she were going to become a pirate. *Let the stars be your guide, your sweat and blood and tears be your ocean …and your hard work be your wind.* Her father's words brought her comfort. She put a hand in her pocket, feeling the dial that was there, that the strange man had left. And suddenly, her tears were no more. What she had seen last night was not a dream. It was real. She didn't care what they thought. She was doing this for her.

She was going to be a time pirate, down to the date.

***

Thunder rolled and lightning flashed once more as Jason returned to Lucy's world.

He was still shaking his head at the oddest conversation he'd had with Little Lucy just a few moments ago, still a bit woozy from the temporal displacement. It had been a quick hop back to his ship, a course correction, and a hop here.

Whenever here was.

The time-trip had been a bit disorientating, as it always was, but since it was the same Earth and same timeline as before, it wasn't as bad as other, less savory journeys across larger divergences.

Still, the dizziness was a bit more than he expected.

A walk in the park, he decided. Nothing to cause worry.

He motioned to two of his crew, Potsdam giants stolen from Frederick Wilhelm's personal collection, who flanked him upon exiting the portal. Though he didn't expect this trip to be fraught with risks, he wanted to be prepared, lest the currents wash him onto strange shores again.

Like it or not, he had been vulnerable with the little girl. Caught off-guard. She had been chatty, curious even, and he liked the spark she had. He wondered if she would even remember their conversation or if she would just pass it off as a dream... He shrugged it off, nodding to his escorts. He was close to the painting – and a very large sum of money – that would shortly be within his grasp.

The large and vacant studio he found himself in was perfectly in keeping with the abode of an artist. Airy, with tall windows to let in light all around. Lamps hung from rafters. Concrete flooring and cork wallboard completed the interior. But where was everything?

The room was empty where there should have been easels and canvases and paints of all kinds and colors all around. He'd seen Da Vinci's studio and had marveled at the mess. Somewhere, he was sure his footprint was in a Pollock painting. But Lucille Sharvet was said to have stood above the rest.

Follow Your Star.

Where was the masterpiece that was said to have been inspired by a father's words?

Where was the girl he had just met, now grown? She'd be in her prime, having just finished her greatest work. His chronometer should have led him straight to her. He gave it a good bump.

This was proving to be a headache.

"Lucille?" Jason searched, calling out her name. Still, nothing – until he caught the edge of a shadow.

"I told you, I hate that name." A girl, no, a woman – the girl was gone – sauntered over from a darkened corner. She was tall, brown hair in a bun and dressed in a tight blue bodysuit, reinforced just like his. Lithe and sharp, she sliced through the warehouse toward him like a knife in the dark. "October 24th, 2040. Right on time."

He looked into her eyes, seeing the same little girl he had seen moments before, though these eyes were fiercer now. A warrior's eyes. "Little Lucy?"

"No. Not anymore," she answered. She looked him over, up and down, staring intently at his face. "You're not as tall as last time. Not what I expected." She placed a hand on her hip, possessing a ravenous confidence that he couldn't help admiring. Who cares about some painting? This was so much better.

"Well," he said, trying to regain some swagger. "You've certainly grown. You're not exactly what I expected either."

"People change." She held out a dial.

For a moment, he didn't recognize it. But as he felt around his waist for his pressure gauge, he realized what she had. Then, it hit him. *I did this. I changed her fate.* "So, no paintings, then? What about *Follow Your Star?* It's supposed to be a priceless work." He rubbed his fingers together, greedily, pining after his lost treasure, hopeful in his newfound one.

She shrugged, indifferently. "I am what I wanted to be."

"And what is that?" He steeled himself, knowing the answer, beckoning his guards closer.

"A time pirate."

Jason struggled against laughing. He thought perhaps he might take her onboard, show her around. But taking her on as part of his crew – well – perhaps he shouldn't have said anything to her when she had been younger, just a moment ago. He should have kept his mouth shut, and just fought it out with her father. He'd have to remember that for next time.

"You can't be a time pirate," he let her know. As she had done moments before to him, he turned the tables by asking: "Where's your time ship? Where's your chronometer? Where's your crew?"

"Ricardo," Lucy called out. From the rafters, a dozen men and women descended from ropes, as if they were pirates plundering a ship.

They were, he realized. His ship. His treasure.

Jason jerked up, aghast, the blood draining from his face. She was serious. *Dangerous.* He had just stumbled out of an innocent girl's room and into a spider's web. And it was all his fault. *Oh god, what did I say to her?*

Now, he laughed, nervously, "That's such a very pirate thing to do."

It was over before it began. His two guards lay unconscious on the floor, taken by surprise. The thin point of a blade pressed painfully against his neck, held firmly by the man she called Ricardo.

Clever girl, indeed. Lucy didn't just want to join his crew. She wanted it all for herself, and she had spent the last twenty years, moments for him, figuring out just how to do it. He might say he was in love, if he knew he would survive the night.

She stretched herself over to him, like a cat creeping ever closer to its prey. She plucked the device out from his hands. "Looks like I have a crew, a chronometer, and soon, a ship." She patted his chest, like one might address a pet.

What have I done?

"Thank you," she told him. "For everything." Jason remained speechless, searching for some way to fix his mistake, knowing *he* was now the treasure, the prize Lucy had sought for twenty years to the night.

Captain Lucy, time pirate, turned to her crew and said, with a cunning, sharp smile, "Let's go get us a Rex."

End.

Notes for Lost Treasure

This story is dedicated to the memory of Lucy Sharvet.
Another, slightly different version of this story, found in *Tales from the Pirate's Cove* from Inklings Press is dedicated to the memory of her sister, Cecilia Sharvet.

Both are true lost treasures.

A Hard Day Hunting Dinosaurs

The creature, quick and birdlike, darted beneath the underbrush. My eyes swept toward it. I took a cautious step closer. Even as a juvenile, my prey was lethal. Just under waist high, flat brown and green mottled feathers blended in and around the bushes and foliage of the late Mesozoic. A perfect camouflage.

I scanned ahead, eliminating my prey's possible hiding spots. While this was my first-time hunting Tyrannosaur, it wasn't my first-time hunting dinosaurs. I had grown tired of setting lazy traps for Triceratops and snares for Stegos. I'd chased down the faster ostrich-like creatures and outwitted packs of raptors — movies made them out to be far more fearsome than the average turkey. In fact, most of the ones I'd brought back to Earth Prime to sell as steaks and burgers were no larger than a Butterball. A disappointment to say the least. I wanted something *bigger*.

Oh well. I'd bag this tiny T-Rex, head back to my beat-up transport truck. Punch in the dial for my return trip home and try another Mesozoic-era Earth in the morning. Dinosaur hunting wasn't as lucrative as it used to be. Too many of us out here doing it now. Most folks back on Earth Prime could order a Bronto-burger at their local drive-thru. But it paid the bills, and it was interesting Earth-hopping, seeing all these other Earths in their infancy. We could do whatever we wanted. It wasn't going to mess with *our* timeline.

The juvenile Tyrannosaur let out a noise somewhere between a choked chirp and a growl. I suppose it was transitioning from weening off its mom to learning how to be a little dinosaur. But it must have gotten caught in something. Low bellows turned into cries. Luckily, I was there to put an end to its distress.

The Rex's calls lured me on. Brushing branches from my face, I followed the pleas into the foliage. She was laying on her side, entangled in roots and branches, feathers flapping wildly. Females had almost no color to them. And they were larger, fiercer than their male counterparts. She ripped and tore at her bindings. I almost felt bad as I raised my rifle.

It was the smell of decomposing meat that gave away my error. I probably should have kept a closer eye on my surroundings. I was tired and distracted. It'd been a long day and I wanted to go home, crash on the couch, and watch my hometown ball players give lessons on how to lose badly.

At first, I thought the foul, decaying smell might mean we were near the little creature's nest. That made sense. She sensed danger and was running home to mommy.

No. If I was near the nest, the smell would permeate the air with a sickly, sweet aroma of raw meat and flesh. Instead, the foulness came in waves, hot and sticky. The branches were still except for where the juvenile thrashed about. There was no wind. Where was that movement of air coming from?

The creature settled down and hopped easily and effortlessly out from the tangle of plants and scooted away. Not a feather was ruffled. *The little bastard tricked me.*

It turned out I wasn't the only hunter here. I hit my emergency alert button as hard and as quick as I could and breathed a sigh of relief when I felt the reassuring buzz signaling that the message had been sent.

My message would reach Earth Prime, and a team of rescuers would track my location and arrive five minutes before my stupid, stupid mistake to prevent me from making it. Sure, it would cost a fortune, and I'd have to pull in twice as much for a while to stay afloat, but at least I'd be alive. I wouldn't be watching ballgames anytime soon. I grunted in disproval. It was my own damned fault.

But that timeline didn't exist yet. For now, I'd have to see this one through. The large Tyrannosaur poked its blood-soaked snout out, exposing teeth long and sharp and jagged enough where I hoped it would be over soon, yet I knew I'd feel *everything* in the first few terrifying moments until I finally succumbed to shock or exsanguination.

The mother dinosaur had been so still. So peaceful. It was a good arrangement. Let her helpless daughter lure in the food, and then momma would take the prey down. Only, I was the prey and I had fallen for it. I guess when there's a failsafe like time-travel, it dulls down the instinct to survive. There's little need to be careful. *But I should. Oh, I should be very careful next time*. This was going to hurt. This was going to hurt so much.

The Tyrannosaur lunged.

End.

Notes for A Hard Day Hunting Dinosaurs

A Hard Day Hunting Dinosaurs was originally recorded for Space Cowboy Book's debut 'Simultaneous Times' podcast, with original music by RedBlackBlueSilver.

Bronto-burger or Stego-steaks anyone?

Forgotten

In life, I was a phantom; in death, I lived. When my sister died, a part of me did too. Before, I had wanted to teach. The future was bright. After her death, I retreated into darkness. My only aim was to get through the day and let my life slip past as fast as time allowed.

I was eight when my parents woke me in the middle of the night and told me Vera was dead. She'd died in an accident. Dad later left and drowned himself in moonshine. Mom got sick. There was no money for me, I had only the mine in the mountain. I slunk away in the deep, disappearing into nothingness – an invisible pick, chipping away. To most, the world is black and white. It was all dark to me. I was just an echo, rippling underground.

I grumbled a 6am greeting as I trudged the hill toward the main driftmouth to meet my other two co-workers. They were among the many milling about before the bell began. Tim spit a stream of chew in response. He even missed my shoes this time. I think he was warming up to me. Though I occasionally chewed myself, my can of Cope tucked away in my coveralls was mostly for him.

He was a big guy, and baggy overalls added to his girth. I don't think he shaved but once or twice a week and washed his oily hair just as infrequently. He shoved it all under a Steelers cap until it was time to switch out for a hardhat. "Why get dolled up for darkness?" He once told me. He wrote poetry in the mornings instead of showering, to combat the dull, mindlessness of the day ahead. It wasn't bad. Something told me in another life, he and Thoreau would have gotten along grand.

Steve ambled over to nod a greeting in between heavy snorts. His nose was red and raw, but not from the mountain chills. Underneath a red-knit cap was a broken man. A war vet, he'd received a limp in his left leg. Vicodin helped him through the pain. The mine was the only job he could get after his discharge, though he joked that it was just until he made it big with his guitar and his band. Adderall helped him through the drudgery of the day. Before I met him, I had no idea you could crush the tablets up and snort both medications at the same time.

After we entered the driftmouth, we waited our turn for the lift that would lower us to our tunnel. When it arrived, all three of us smacked the wall above our heads, leaving greasy handprints along with all the others. I guess it was our way of leaving something behind should we never rise back out of the black.

I could have sworn I heard my sister's voice in the back of my head. Occasionally, I'd hear her, like echoes hitting my subconscious. I could never understand what she was saying, only the still softness of it.

"You all right there, Vic?" Tim asked.

"Yeah," I returned, hoping to channel my fatigue into my words to play off the unsettling moment of Vera's voice. I'd stayed up late the night before, as I often did, reading books. I was on a Rome kick lately.

"Get yer head into the game, son." Tim shook his own. "It's dangerous down there."

"Sure."

We walked the rest of the way, about a mile or so, in silence. The tiny room where we mined was connected to wider, mostly lit paths. In the main tunnels, the mine was clean and clear of dust. It wasn't until you weaved through miles of mine to fresher veins that the old image of cramped, cold voids came true. Our LED lamps were our only weapons against the black. That, and our wit. It was just us in our room with our seam under the massive mountain of loose drift above.

As usual, through the din of hammers, our work devolved into heated discussions over the mundane. Tim would no doubt diss some football team that did Pittsburg wrong. And Steve would bring up his cat. *That damned cat.*

"Whiskers caught himself a robin this morning," Steve said through more snorts. "Saw the whole thing. Crept behind a bush, leapt and pinned the bird down. Left it for me on the porch. Sweet cat."

I loved birds. I tolerated cats. Hearing Whisker's latest horror story added to the dreariness of the day. *I hate the dark. The drugs. That everyone assumed we were some back-wood hicks hell-bent on destroying the planet with our coal.* I just wanted a full fridge, a cold home-brew, and a thorough book on the Civil War to fall asleep with. *So much for being a teacher.*

I could never afford to be one now, between the rising costs of college and the low entry-level pay. I gave up on that dream long ago. Coal mining was honest work, but we only illuminated the home; teachers illuminate the soul.

"Would you shut up about the cat?" I asked. I always asked.

"In this life, Vic," Steve chuckled, "you're either the cat or the canary."

Seeing how we were in the mines, it wasn't hard to guess which ones we were. I shot him a bird of my own, which I'm sure he never saw, hidden as it was in shadow.

From somewhere in the mine, a scoop's engine switched on. The heavy-load tractor vibrated the walls, shook up dust, and penetrated our earplugs. I didn't know where exactly it was in relation to us. Tunnels twisted echoes down here, so that you could never be sure where a sound came from or where it was going. Normally, it didn't matter.

Today, it did. The scoop must have been close. The driver must have knocked into something or scraped a wall and hit a pocket, I don't know. Dust kicked up more than normal, as did my coughing. Walls began to buzz, and drift started to rain.

Steve stood still, though his headlamp rattled along with Tim's. Some said headlamps looked like faint specters in the dust of the mines, others said they looked like life itself, our only respite from the inescapable darkness, as if it were God and He was everywhere. To me, the rattling headlights screamed a warning.

Tim spread his feet apart and bent low to keep balanced as the shaking started. Coal dust blanketed the room and swallowed our light. Heavier clumps of coal and rock fell in on us. I could make out individual bits as they cascaded past my flickering lamp. Every step I took along with Tim and Steve out of the room was eternal. I endured lifetimes of terror.

"Get out!" Tim shoved between Steve and I, knocking the injured veteran aside; Steve's chances of survival dropped to zero. I tried to help him, but I too lost my sure footing in the helter-skelter of the collapsing cave.

I caught hold of Tim's slack coveralls. "Get back here and help!" Tim broke free and tried to escape. I reached out to Steve. He held my hand tight as I pulled him back, grunting with exertion.

Tim turned and stared at the two of us, his expression ghostly, "It's already too late."

He was right. If he had been just a moment faster, he probably would have made it before the roof caved in. If I hadn't slowed him, or if he had reacted quicker, he'd have escaped.

Instead, rocks piled at the junction with all of us on the wrong side. It continued to rain, not only blocking our escape, but burying us within. I couldn't breathe. I couldn't see. My heart was burning in my chest with fire. I tried to swallow my fear, but all I managed to do was to black out.

I came to with Tim tapping on my shoulder. I hacked out a throaty, thick film of dark phlegm before I could respond. "I'm okay, but where's Steve?"

"Don't talk," he huffed. "No air." He wiped away another layer of film from his light and pointed it at Steve. While we were mostly buried and constricted to just a few feet of space, Steve was crushed. We could see a leg, broken and bloody, and a hand, sticking out of the silt. The rest we chose to ignore.

We kept silent, waiting for help. I thought I heard voices, but I could not tell where they were coming from or how close they were. One voice tugged at the back of my head. It sounded like my sister's.

The coal was crushing us; the air thin, full of carbon dioxide and dust. When we breathed, we coughed. I could tell Tim was fading.

"One last piece, Vikkie," Tim strained to ask. My sister called me that. Tim never did. Though it was strange, I let it go. With some time and effort, I managed to dig out the can of chew from my front pocket. I figured I owed it to him, since I had stopped him to save Steve. He wouldn't be here if it wasn't for me.

He never once mentioned this. Perhaps he felt guilty about running. Instead, he spoke some of his poetry through chaw and coughs. "Though our lives were forgotten ones, we beseech thee, do the dead affect the living, do we keep on, once we are gone?"

I hope he got a good chaw going before he died.

After I was sure he'd gone, I took the can back. "Thanks," I said as I tried to keep myself sane, death staring at me through the darkness. I drifted off with my mouth full of nicotine and my head full of Tim's words of an empty life I never lived, wondering just how quickly I'd be forgotten too.

"*It's time, Vikkie,*" a voice said. I was pretty sure it wasn't a mine worker come to rescue me. In fact, I was pretty sure I was already dead.

"*Follow me,*" Vera's voice continued.

In my memories, her face is covered in red spots. I assumed it was normal, not that she had rosacea. When I was six, in our treehouse, I'd poke and pick at them like they were strawberries. She'd giggle. It was innocent at the time. I couldn't see those deep red splotches on her faceless voice now, but I was sure it was her. Who else would care I was dead? *Was I dead?*

"*Yes.*"

The answer didn't frighten me as much as I expected. I was more curious than concerned. "You aren't here," I said, looking around.

Technically, neither are you.

"Fair point." I felt like just a voice, a drifting echo. Everything shut out but for our voices.

"*Now it's time to come join me.*"

"I don't want to go." I'd never lived. It would have been nice to experience life before I left. The mine was dark and distant. A door opened, white and crackling with energy. "You want me to take this door, and join you?"

"*No. Follow my voice. Ignore the door.*"

"What is it? What's on the other side?"

"Temptation. That path is perilous, little brother. You should come home with me."

Vera was right, I was sure. It was safe, she was someone I could trust. The unknown is never certain. I followed her voice as the world I left behind went black and the door began to shrink away.

No. I'm not done yet. I've always taken the safe route. The mine offered security and safety but look where that landed me. Tim's poem hit me once more. I was gone. Most likely, I was already forgotten. I strayed from the voice and chose to take the white doorway. It grew as I approached, enveloping me. Suddenly, I was surrounded by white light and a searing hot pain.

"Beware, little brother. Life is brutish."

Gunfire erupted nearby. As the echoes of the blast dissipated, the white-hot light diminished. The brightness was the setting sun. The scent was of pine mixed with acrid smoke. The scene coalesced. I heard cries for help over the sound of rushing water.

Another burst of gunfire. It wasn't a single shot from a .22 or another dinky pea-shooter, rather the crack of something big. A whole lot of something big. Black powder, maybe? As the reverberation of thunder weakened with each concussion wave, it was replaced by moaning, and then silence.

"Where am I?"

"Earth. Sometime in the past. I'm not sure of the rest, though I'd hazard you're near a battle."

"I- I time-traveled?"

"That's one way to put it. You're dead and no longer bound by physical restrictions and constructs like time. Even still, you're not supposed to be here."

"I want to go check it out." I wondered where in history I'd landed. Sometime where black powder was in use, I gathered. I drifted toward the sounds of violence, anxiously anticipating my discovery, basking in the sunlight and fresh air. I was a ghost, and everything I'd heard about them were wrong. I felt everything. I felt *alive*.

"You need to leave. I'm not supposed to be here either, but I'll stay as long as I can. If you make this journey, be prepared to do it alone."

I could feel a shadow creep over me, like a black blanket. I pushed it aside and kept going. "I'm a ghost. Like you said, they can't hurt me. I'll be fine."

"That's not what I'm afraid of. There's something I must tell you about what you're doing. The dead can still affect the living."

"What are you so worried about? Aren't you the one who used to tell me there's no such thing as ghosts?" I half-hopped, half-floated over the hill, an astronaut on an unfamiliar Earth.

At the crest of a bluff, I could make out the whole battle below. Before me was the red, blue, and white of a Yankee flag hanging limply from a fallen fort. Rises on other side were lined with marksmen shooting down into the fray. Men in grubby grey uniform shoved their way through the fort with their bayonets, skewering any who stood in their way. On one side of the fort, a gunboat sat quiet on the river, as wounded soldiers in blue sought safety in the river, only to drown or be ignored by the silent ship.

It was a field of forgotten souls. *This wasn't a fort. And this isn't a battle. It's a massacre and this is one giant grave.* I hurried down into the carnage.

Fort Pillow. It was one of the only engagements in American history between the War of 1812 and the Korean War where roughly an even number of both black and white troops fought and died side by side. The Confederates wouldn't stand such an abomination, particularly so close to Lincoln's Emancipation, and they set to wipe them off the map. They succeeded.

"You would have made a fine teacher," Vera said.

"I can talk to the history, yes," I answered in a low, solemn voice. "But can I convince anyone to not make the same mistakes?"

Yankee soldiers, both white and black, lay wounded and dead before me. Those who still lived loaded their Lorenzes. Several succeeded in pointing them in the general direction of the Rebels. Most did not. All of them were cut down by rebel gunfire or bayonet, even the ones surrendering. They were made to stand, then they were shot.

A rider on horseback appeared through the thick smoke growing over the fort. The rider was dressed in full uniform. In his belt, he carried both a small dragoon pistol and a sword. But in his hands, he carried a large wooden pike. *He must be here to declare victory,* I thought.

His horse trotted past several wounded white soldiers until he arrived at a groaning black one, blood smeared across his face. Despite his wounds, he was still trying to scoot away on his back, digging his heels in the dirt, pushing away from the rider, heading toward the false safety of the river. He was not fast enough. The rider pounded the pike through the chest of the man. The soldier gasped and gurgled blood, then died.

While the rebels picked through the white soldiers, relieving them of their jackets, belt buckles, boots, and lives, the rider continued singling out black soldiers and then running them through with his pike.

"How can this happen? Lives wasted…"

"Most of us are already ghosts long before we are dead. Life is unfair that way."

I couldn't accept it. I forced my way through the field of corpses, the look of defeat etched into their vacant eyes. I turned against the death and headed for a soldier still alive, stumbling over his fallen friends to escape the Devil on horseback.

"Not everyone can be saved, little brother. Not even me. Come home, please. You don't need to be here to hear the truth. I'll tell you everything. Just come with me."

I ignored Vera. Her words didn't make any sense.

The escaping soldier turned, ashen-faced, forehead sweaty with blood trailing down his left leg. The rider was closing the distance, but I'd managed to place myself between them. I knew it wouldn't do any good, the rider would pass right through me, but I did it anyway.

Behind me, my sister called, *"You're a ghost, Vikkie! You can't help them. That's my fault. I made you what you are."*

I stopped. A chill rippled through me. I don't know how. "What do you mean?"

The soldier kept sliding down the pile of corpses and the rider kept coming – until his horse stopped. The horse reared and neighed, the rider thrown from the saddle, landing with a crunch of bones in the pile of bodies as the horse galloped away.

My focus returned to the soldier, who caught a second wind at his bit of fortune. The river was just within reach. Somehow it worked. If he could make it to the edge, he could fall in, and hope for…

What?

Black powder ripped through the air once more. The soldier stiffened as if stung through his spine. The soldier, in his Yankee uniform, fell to the ground, lifeless. I jerked toward the rider, who'd recovered from his fall and on one knee, had drawn his pistol.

Vera was right. I couldn't save him. That's no surprise. I couldn't save myself. I couldn't even save her. The corpses filled my eyes until I could bear to look no longer. "These people didn't want to be here. They never had a choice; it was the only option open to them."

"It's like you in the mine after my death, isn't it?" she prompted. "You had no choice, and then it killed you."

"Yes." Her words haunted me. I didn't want to admit it to her. But there was no escaping the truth. Her death destroyed my life. If she hadn't died, mom and dad would still be together. I would have gone to college. Most importantly, my sister would be with me, instead of some voice pulling at me. Yet she *had* died. And so had I. I knew all this, but none of it was Vera's fault.

I floated away from the soldiers on the fallen field, weighed down by failure. "What do you want me to do?"

"Allow me to direct you to the other side."

There was something with the way she phrased it, a wrong word rubbing over a raw wound. "And if I don't?"

"If you continue your journey, you may fade out of existence too, like a forgotten memory, a slain soldier on the losing side of battle."

A crackling doorway of white energy opened before me. I patted down to where my pocket used to be for my can of chew. Of course, it wasn't there. Being dead did have some disadvantages. *Maybe it's time to move on.*

I caught the dead man's eyes once more with my own. "I'm sorry I failed you."

Vera placed herself between me and the exit, her consciousness a wall. *"Failing is a fact of life."*

Her words rubbed me raw, in the way only a sibling can do. I pushed through her voice, angrily. "I'm not alive. I never was." I made my way through the searing pain of the door.

"Wait!"

I went from the fort to a barren outcrop of rock. A thin wisp of decay hung in the air. The day was fading fast. Around the barren pit of rocks, groves of mangled trees stood like temple walls around a single stone in the middle. On the rock was a smear of red. Etched into it was the single eagle of Rome.

My sister followed me. I wanted to be by myself. It was like we were kids again and she wouldn't stay out of my room.

"You must come home now. I'm not sure how much longer I can stay."

"Then leave," I huffed. "I am home." I've always loved reading about Rome. Maybe I *could* make my home here. "Why don't you just leave me alone?"

"I haven't left you since I died."

I knew it was true, I knew she had been there. Just as she could push my buttons to anger, she also knew just what to say and how to say it so that I would calm down. It must have been a trick she learned to keep herself out of trouble with mom. "You were always the smart one. It was your death that made me want to become a teacher."

"I know."

I frowned, "but it was also your death that made Dad leave. After he left, I had no choice but to work in the mine. In a way, your death killed me too."

"I'm sorry, little brother. I never meant to hurt you."

"What do you mean?"

The sound of rustling branches of the nearby bushes turned my attention away. At twilight, a man approached the hidden grove. He carried a bundle in his arms. The thickets and gnarled trees stirred once more. The man with the bundle was not alone. There was something else. *I hate the dark.*

"You don't know what happened, do you? I thought you might have come to realize the truth on your own. That's part of the reason I'm here. To make amends. I just didn't realize it would be so hard for me, how painful."

"Pain should end at death," I said. For my sister and I, it hadn't. For some of us, pain started from the day we are born, through no fault of our own.

"Pain is a part of us. For some, it defines us."

My attention was diverted back to the Roman. He was at the bloodied rock, setting a bundle down. *What is he doing?* The bundle wriggled and let out a cry. "There's a baby in there…"

I felt crushed once more. Who could allow such a thing? I pulled myself through the air over to the baby in the bundle and that's when I knew. The baby girl had a cleft above her upper lip, splitting it in two. But she was still a human being. In Roman times, leaving deformed babies out in the woods for wolf food was as casual for them as condoms were for us.

The man left her there, just as I figured he would, and crept away.

I thought back to the rosacea on my sister's face. It had always just been there. I occasionally picked at it, but I was just a little brother annoying his big sister. It wasn't done with any spite. The way she giggled when I did it, I thought it was fun.

"Once, I saw you come crying home, rushing to your bedroom. I watched tears splash on the wooden steps." The realization swallowed me. "How many times did you come running home like that?"

"Many times, Victor, many more than I could bear."

She was right. "I never thought about how you must have dealt with all the teasing while alone at school." Memories were becoming clear to me, as if I remembered something I'd long left to the deep mines of my mind. "And you?" I rippled with unease, like a wave rolling back out to sea. "What really happened?"

I wanted the truth, the answers I already knew, but confronting them would have to wait. "That Roman ruin of a man is leaving his daughter…"

"It's the way of things."

Out of the woods, not one, not two, but five sets of yellow eyes glowed from gnarl of roots. The wolves smelled their next meal. They knew the routine. They sniffed the heavy air towards the rock and stalked toward the baby.

"Do something!"

"I thought you said this was natural?"

"I was wrong. We have to fight against nature."

"I don't know what you want me to do, Vera. In case you don't remember, I couldn't help the soldier, how can I help now?"

"It was the rider you couldn't control. You scared the horse."

I replayed the events from earlier. I had felt a surge of emotion charge through when the horse panicked. *Was that me?*

There was only one way to find out. I waved frantically, shooing, yelling, putting myself between the baby and the pack while my sister joined in shouting. I thought I saw a few ears perk up, but they continued to approach the rock, growling with bare teeth.

"It's not working."

"I hadn't noticed. What do you want me to do?"

"I don't know. It worked before."

The pack crept closer, the biggest one leaped upon the stone slab, the baby in reach of its jaws.

"Wait! How did you feel right before the horse?"

"Confusion," I thought back. "But then something else, as if I were remembering something. I felt... shock. Anger."

I knew the answer, though I was no actor. I couldn't just conjure strong emotions. Still, I yelled at the closest wolf with all the passion I could muster. It stopped, and looked at me, but the others came closer. The leader of the pack turned back toward the baby, the girl's deformed lips undulating with every cry that might carry her last breath.

Her dad left her to die. I tried to channel the anger for my own father, but it didn't seem personal enough.

"It's not our dad you should be mad at."

"Now's not the time for family reflection," I said, struggling to wrap myself around any emotion strong enough to frighten away the wolves. "Think of something, tell me what really happened with you. I mean, I know. I think I know, but—"

"I killed myself."

"Why?" My voice dropped. The wolves stopped.

"You know."

"Because of the way others treated you. Because your face looked different from theirs. Because of something you could not control."

"Yes."

"Our lives were ruined because bullies couldn't stop long enough to get to know how beautiful you really were?"

The wolves backed away from the white-hot intensity I emanated. If I could have let out tears, I would have. We were no different than the Romans, only we waited until kids were old enough to see the wolves coming.

"I couldn't handle the teasing anymore. It wasn't just at school. It was on my computer, my phone, I couldn't escape it until I made it go away."

"And Dad?"

"I tried to tell him about it. The last time, he was working late, pulling a second shift to put back money for my school. He was tired. And he told me to "man up" before he slipped off to sleep. It was the last straw. I was so angry and depressed and tired. I couldn't handle it anymore. I wanted to disappear. So I did."

That explained so much. The guilt of my father, the sudden remodel of the upstairs bathroom, the way everyone hushed when I was around. It was too easy to dismiss me back then. I was so young, so lost, so forgotten.

I looked down at the screaming baby, her voice cracking and gurgling, fighting to be heard with all her meek little might. *There needed to be some compassion in this world, for there was none in the next. This world is all that matters.*

"Stop," I roared to the wolves, the fury rising in every ethereal fiber I could bring to bear. It was all I could do to scream, but I managed a haunting, howling, "get away from her!"

"Something's happening, Vikkie. You're glowing."

I could see myself in shimmering light. It felt like a warming ray of sun hitting just right on a cloudy day. Only, I was the ray. My luminescence sparked against the cold grey of night, and the wolves stopped, turned away from the baby girl, and whimpered as they scooted away.

I looked down at the girl, and her blue eyes smiled back at me.

The father crept cautiously from the safety of his hiding place among a set of trees, back toward the rock, as if unsure what to do. He looked down at his girl, returned her smile, and scooped her up. He met my eyes with his and exclaimed, *"Mirabilia!"* before scurrying off with his daughter clutched tightly in both arms. I got the feeling he would never let her go again.

My light dimmed, and the world turned dark.

I wanted to turn to my sister, to congratulate her and to share in some of her pain. We had done it. I could picture the two of us traveling time together, righting wrongs, changing history. I was happy for the first time in years.

Yet, there was growing emptiness where I'd felt Vera before, as if she were being pulled away. I looked around for her, frantic. She was already disappearing. To where, to what end, I did not know. I called to her, "Don't leave, not yet! We have so much to do."

"It's time for you to save yourself. My path is different now, as is yours. Do not become a forgotten one in death, Victor. I love you."

"Vera?"

I didn't want to be there anymore. Like the upstairs bathroom must have felt for my mother, this place was too full of emotion. I needed an escape. A door opened in front of me. I forced myself through, despite the pain.

There was nothing on the other side. I drifted in the dark with no frame of reference to ground me. Surrounded by emptiness, truly invisible. I tried to scream. It came out as only a whimper. I urged myself onward, desperate for a door, finding none. I hated the dark, the pressing silence, being alone. Long corridors of nothingness stretched on forever.

My sister had been right. Life was brutish. Life was unfair. One could rage against it all one liked and still fall victim to it, like those soldiers at Fort Pillow. Or one could become a canary to the cats of the world, like the little girl. Like my sister.

And then there were those caught in the middle. I *could* have been a teacher. But I went with the flow. Coal mining was honest work. There's nothing wrong with it. But it wasn't what I *wanted* to do with my life. *I should have fought harder. I may still have failed, but at least I would have tried. I might have even succeeded.*

It was a good lesson to learn, I admit. But a bit late for me, lost in the darkness that I was. My miserable existence continued until I stumbled upon a light at the end of a long passageway. *Where had that come from? Is it a doorway?*

When I, after an age, finally reached it, I saw that it was not a doorway, but instead, a dimly lit light bulb. At first, I did nothing. It was blinding. As I grew accustomed to brightness, as I began to see, I began to understand. *I know that light.*

I was not lost. I'd never been. I'd been in my mountain, my mine, all this time. I followed the usual route from the bulb to a junction. On my right, down the tunnel, was where I'd died.

I could go down that route. At the other fork, however, a searing, crackling door emerged, ringed in lightning and flame. I could pass through it, escape this mountain despite the sure pain I knew it would bring. But I would be free. I had no idea what to expect at the end of the tunnel.

The odds that I could change my fate were impossible. Escape was my only realistic option. I drifted toward the doorway, stopping to say goodbye to my mine and what might have been.

Do not become a forgotten one. My sister's words echoed underground. She may have left, but her words were with me. Tim's question in his poem came to mind. Can the dead affect the living? Vera said that they did. And she was right. *She was always right.*

I turned away from the doorway and sure freedom to step into the unknown, pushing my way down the tunnel toward LED-lit hardhats at the end. The shadows underneath looked slightly altered, but I could make out three familiar figures.

I recognized Steve first because of his limp. What was odd was a cage holding a hurt pigeon, mottled in grey-white. Mines had no use for birds anymore, but here it was like a damned mascot. It looked like it escaped a near-death brush with a cat. *Maybe it survived Whisker's clutches?* One wing was mangled, but the bird seemed very much alive and happy – for a bird in a cage, in a mine.

"Whiskers tried to hurt this poor fella this morning," Steve said without a single snort. "Saw the whole thing from my window. Crept behind a bush and got it. Couldn't leave him alone to die."

"That's cute about the bird," I heard myself, my corporeal-self, say.

"Hey, in this life, you're either the cat or the canary. But sometimes, all the canary needs is a little bit of help. The bird's like me," Steve went on, "I have this limp from the war. Someone saved me, pushed me away when I could have been killed."

"That's great," Tim said. "I brought a bird of my own, want to see it?"

I knew where this was going. More importantly, I knew what was about to happen. The roar of the scoop's motor switched on. Walls began to vibrate. As always, time was against me. If I could not figure out a way to get them to clear the room, then I would watch them, and myself, die.

The bird. It seemed restless with the thunder of the motor, but otherwise quiet. I slammed myself into it. The cage rattled and the bird chirped. One, lonely, pitiful chirp.

"What was that?" Tim asked.

Steve chuckled. "Looks like that bird of mine isn't a fan of the scoop."

No, you fools. Don't downplay this. You're all going to die. I scared a horse. I'd run off the wolves. I was reasonably sure I could excite a small bird.

I hoped.

I sensed the cave about to collapse, but the bird settled back down.

Sometimes you must fight to be heard. Sometimes, even when you did your best, you were as loud as you could, it was still as if you were silent. *I was going to be heard.*

The bird looked at me and not through me. It began chirping like mad. Its tiny mangled wing fluttered and it fell from its perch which only made it bounce around even more.

The three of them went still.

"The gas sensors aren't going off," my corporeal self said.

"Doesn't matter. Something spooked this bird and I don't want to be here to find out what. Even if it's nothing I want to get the guy settled. You guys should follow." Steve took his bird-cage and started out of the room.

The room began to rumble. The mine shook, and the first rocks fell.

I was too late. "Get out!" I yelled. I was surprised to hear my voice. My living counterpart had screamed the words too. *Was there enough time?*

Steve obliged, limping through the long passage. The last time this happened, Tim had shoved his way through and knocked us down. I'd gone back to help Steve, pulling Tim back, effectively killing him.

This time, Steve was halfway down the tunnel and I was behind Tim. He was the point of safety. But there was no getting past him. *He was the cat.*

Drift began to clog the passage, pieces rained, the tunnel cracked, and the room was filling fast.

Tim tumbled in the darkness.

Though he fell, I thought he would claw himself up and out, even if it meant trampling over my corporeal-self. I saw him grab onto me and I knew it was over. My spirit sank. I prepared for death to come once more and for the cycle to repeat.

Tim grabbed me and pushed me ahead. "Go, now!"

I saw concern sweep across my face – a moment of hesitation – before my corporeal self tried to pull him up. He resisted. "Don't be forgotten."

With one final look back, I watched myself duck through the last of the portal to safety as the cave closed around him and his outstretched arm. I watched myself recover, and with a look of surprise and shock, pull on his arm. It was no use. I knew he'd suffer under there, if the heavy rock hadn't crushed him already. He'd sacrificed himself for me.

This time around, some of us survived. Steve and his bird were safe. And so was I. A moment later, the rest of the tunnel closed in, and Tim was gone.

I wanted to thank him, to mourn him. To let him know, despite all the misery in the world, we can use the pain to push us ahead or pin us back, and he, somehow in this changed timeline, made the choice to use his pain to push me forward. I would not forget him, and I would make sure no one else did either.

I wanted to say all those things, and more, to ask Vera if she found her peace, but it was time for me to leave. I felt a tug on my consciousness. I knew what was happening, my body was calling me home.

There was another pull. I was jerked back, yanked with all the might of an exploding supernova ripping me out of whatever this existence was. It hurt. The agony continued as the forces at work shoved me back into my shell. No living being would have survived this. Fortunately, I was not alive.

Not yet.

End.

My favorite show growing up was *Quantum Leap*. Scott Bakula as do-gooder Sam Beckett leaping from one good deed to another, rewriting history, improving lives, made for a delightful show. Sam (assisted by his friend, Al) made you think, laugh, cry and sometimes cringe (there's certain episodes we don't talk about). Among the more entertaining episodes was my favorite with Stephen King. "The Boogieman" where Sam tests wits with… the devil? Aside from its camp the episode is unusual in that it infuses a healthy dose of horror.

Forgotten was really my attempt at writing *Quantum Leap* with the same idea. I don't think I hit the same heights as the show, most notably because I don't have Dean Stockwell. Just as importantly, *Quantum Leap* worked best when it went small – focusing on a single character and their needs. With Forgotten, I tried to go big. Too big.

I desperately wanted to sling my Sam around many more eras of history. The first draft had a T-Rex, because -- dinosaurs. And we went to other places. Too many. But smaller is better, just as the original show focused on a single character, a single moment in time. Forgotten would have worked best had it stuck to one divergence that focused on the heart and how saving the girl from the wolves had rippled across time, creating slight changes. As much as I love this story, I feel it's overstuffed and unclear at times. It was certainly a learning experience for me.

But Forgotten still manages to cross one item off my writer's bucket list: to infuse my fandom of *Quantum Leap* with a dose of horror. It's not often done within the context of time-travel (but should be, don't you think?). Perhaps that mash-up is worth digging into – just so long as one does not dig too deep. Who knows what horrors would stir?

Forgotten was originally published in *Tales from the Underground*.

The Terrible Lizard of Holborn Hill

The rank smell of cigars, beer, and sweat, was more Old West than London High Society. It was as if the smoke itself had wafted through an open Chronus Corporation time portal. Gideon Green sniffed. Still, it was better than the shit and piss-filled streets outside. London's sewer system wouldn't even be designed for another ten years.

"Time-travel, they told me. See the past, rescue a few errant dinosaurs. Fun, they said," Gideon not-quite whispered under his breath. His nose wrinkled as he made his way through the club. "They never said how badly the past *smelt*." When he'd signed on for this job, he'd only looked at the promised zeros on the check. The dinosaurs didn't matter. Neither had the idea of time-travel. Now that he was here, wherever here ended up being at the time, he realized there wasn't enough of those nice circular numbers.

"Cool it, Gid." Jill Horner returned, "people are turning their heads at your talk."

The Englishmen were strewn over the club in their chairs like wet towels. Those not invested in their drinks upturned eyebrows toward the two newcomers.

"Me? You're dressed as a man in a Gentleman's club, a look you're not pulling off. They're not looking at me. Let's just mosey on downstairs all relaxed-like, get our dinosaur, and go home. Should be easy." Gideon checked to make sure his taser was secured before heading to the stairs and took another look at his companion. Jill did not pass for a man, even with her hair chopped short — she'd found a knife in the kitchen a few minutes prior and butchered it without hesitation.

But it wasn't her hair that held Gideon's sway; it was her face. She held the look of an excited child in a museum, rushing from one exhibit to another, cheek pressed against glass. She wanted to be here. She was the historian. He just dealt with the dinosaurs. There were no dinosaurs in 1850's London. Well, there wasn't supposed to be. A Chronus Corporation malfunction with the time portal had caused some interesting displacements. This was Jill and Gideon's second mission, having recently recovered an *Ornithomimus* from Feudal Japan.

The further they descended the stairs, the more the ruckus rose to greet them. It reminded Gideon of the sports bar back home in Illinois when his team of choice did their usual job of losing.

The room below was much the same as above, but without its sense of civility. Jackets were thrown about, hands holding wads of notes waved in the air and beers were bumped as bets were made. The crowd made a sloppy semi-circle surrounding a small stage. On it were three above-average sized English bulldogs and—

"A bear?" Gideon asked the air.

Jill responded anyway, "Bear-baiting."

"Yes, but wasn't it outlawed by this time?"

"I suppose when you have enough money," Jill replied, pushing her way through the crowd to get a closer look, "nothing's off the table."

The bear swung a heavy paw at the lunging dog. Gideon assumed the canine would be swatted away. Instead, a chain caught the bear, holding it back as the dog dove in with its teeth. The bear howled. Gideon turned away, facing Jill who kept her eyes on the carnage. Before long, the beast's growls turned to whimpers.

"That was... brutal," Jill said against a rising chorus of "more!" and "the bloody bear's done for!"

The crowd's clamor quieted to hushed whispers as the bear was dragged away and a man robed in gold strode to center stage.

"Gid, are you sure our coordinates and dates are right?"

"The dinosaur arrived a few days before we did. The portals aren't exact, but according to tracking, it should be here—"

"Gentlemen," the announcer interrupted. "We'll give the beast a chance to rest, but don't you worry, we're just getting started. I, Barnum Bakker, present to you something amazing, something never witnessed in London or all the world – you've seen monsters at the Crystal Palace, now – in the flesh, I bring you a creature beyond imagination! Gentleman, place your bets. The bulldog, or terrible bird-lizard?"

"For fuck's sake!" Jill threw an arm out angrily, nearly striking a fat balding man waving a wad of bills.

"It can't be—"

Onto the stage lumbered an odd-looking creature, limping as if it had been drugged. The poor thing appeared as if evolution took a wrong turn somewhere and wound up at a dead end. The head looked like a duck. The legs and tail a lizard, and its torso was feathered in white and bright blue. It was large too. The dinosaur made the bear look like a cute pet. And this was only a juvenile, Gideon knew. *Iguanodon bernissartensis.*

An herbivore from the late cretaceous, Iguanodon had unusual front limbs that were well-suited for walking on all fours. However, the dinosaur could also walk on its hind legs, leaving its most unusual feature open for use – two sharp, bony spikes for thumbs. The earliest fossil finds had only recovered one thumb spike, leading early paleontologists and biologist to reconstruct *Iguanodon* with a single small horn over its nose.

Yet, this juvenile had his thumb-spikes covered in thick, leathery gloves.

"Injured too many of its handlers, you think?" Jill asked.

"Looks like it, but without them, our living, breathing paycheck over there doesn't stand a chance against those dogs."

"What are we going to do?"

"What can we do?" They couldn't just march up on stage, set up the time-device, and flick it on in front of an audience. Though the simplest solution, and it would fatten Gideon's wallet faster, there was nothing like opening a time-portal in the middle of Victorian London to raise a few eyebrows. Pretty sure he'd skimmed over the word 'discrete' a few times in the company handbook.

Of course, there was nothing discrete about what the Chronus Corporation had been up to. Their work in time-travel and general mucking about with Mother Nature had made this mess in the first place. And now here Gideon and Jill were, thrust into the past, correcting the corporation's mistakes.

It was up to them to bring the dinosaur back to the future, back to where it could be poked and prodded and studied. And they had to do it with as few wrinkles to the timeline as they could manage, else they might return to a future not their own. That was also something he'd glanced at in the guidelines. He should have asked for a few mores zeroes on his check.

"Follow me, I have an idea," Gideon said.

The pair made their way to the side of the bricked room as the *Iguanodon* was led to the stage in chains by several burly brutes. In any other circumstance, where the dinosaur wasn't drugged, those men — as muscled as they were – wouldn't have had a prayer in wrangling the creature. Even in its lethargic state, it was clear who held the upper hand.

The crowd continued to gasp. Clearly, they'd never seen anything like it. Even the few that had been to the Crystal Palace and seen the statues and the remains of dinosaurs wouldn't see that this creature in front of them was one of those magnificent, extinct wonders, any more than the creator of the abacus would recognize a calculator. To them, it was just a funny looking thing, probably prodded out of some African jungle or the wild west of the Americas. And that's when the laughter began.

It started as surprise, then as more people let out a guffaw, it grew into a socially acceptable breakdown. Suddenly, a room full of England's elites had thrown themselves to mirth against the poor creature. Even one of the brutes began to chuckle. His hands loosened and the bulldog he held broke loose and dove at the dinosaur. The creature let out a startled yelp as feathers and dander flew into the air.

"Bring back the bear, the dogs don't need a snack!" A man called out to an uproar in response. "My money is on the barkers!"

"Gents," Barnum called, "I assure you that this beast is more than adequate for the challenge." He turned a nervous eye toward another brute and in a whisper demanded: "take the gloves off."

"But sir," Gideon could barely discern the man say, "them spikes. It'll do in the dogs."

"Just see to it."

The brute removed the gloves cautiously, as if he'd seen beforehand just what damage the dinosaur's thumbs could do. Once removed, the brute ducked away.

The *Iguanodon* still reeled from the injury, nursing it between howls of agony and with licks from his purplish-blue tongue. He was too intent on the wound to notice another dog flank him until the dog growled.

The *Iguanodon's* eyes went wide. Chains buckled at the joints along the brick wall. It stood on its hind-legs, stumbled against his wounds. This was a creature that would have faced off against the likes of a *Megalosaurus* or *Tyrannosaur*. A big, beefy bulldog was only a toy, Gideon realized, even if the dogs had gotten its lick in first. He knew what was going to happen even before the dog did.

A flick of the thumb-spike. A yelp. Then… silence.

A hush fell over the crowd, followed by whispers. The poor creature had only meant to defend itself. But now it thrashed against its chains, threatening everyone in the room. The sensible ones swept to the stairs. Others began changing their bets, unaware that they'd be the ones to lose. Bolts and fasteners embedded into the brick that were barely strong enough for a bear buckled under the dinosaur's mass.

Gideon shoved toward a brute, removed his stun gun and drove it under the man's neck. The gun let out a series of sparks and the man went down. "Sorry, needed your keys, and I didn't think you'd just hand them over."

Jill dug through the man's waistcoat until she retrieved them. "This will empty the room in a hurry. You get crowd control, I'll get the dino."

Jill made for the lock, fumbled with it through sweaty palms while Gideon pulled people toward the stairs. Still, more people remained than fled. "It's like no one here has seen *King Kong*," he said.

Jill returned a sour look. "Just clear the room."

The second dog lunged. The Iguanodon swung around, just as Jill loosened the chain, causing a bolt to snap from the brick. The chain bit into a brute, knocking him unconscious as the tail whipped at a second brute's head. The dog scampered off. Neither brute was as lucky.

Barnum Bakker slid off the bottom of his cane to reveal a long, thin blade. He launched it like a javelin, the blade dug into the dinosaur. The creature reared in response and honked out a deep, throbbing call that echoed off the bare walls of the small room. Gideon and Jill covered their ears as it thundered free and stomped around the stage. The whole building shook.

"No, you daft idiot!" Gideon called after Barnum.

Jill was still by the dinosaur, on unsure footing against the shaky floor. The creature's tail swung towards her. Gideon sped through the crowded hall and shoved Jill down on the floor, landing on top of her as the tail swiped over their heads.

"Thank you. Now, get off."

"Don't mention it, we're even now."

"After I saved your ass back in Japan? Jill shook her head, "Nice try."

The dinosaur, on all fours and trailing blood and feathers, careened out of the room in a frightened frenzy A crash amid a jolt of the building told the pair what they did not wish to hear: their dinosaur was now roaming free on the streets of London. They raced after it.

"Bloody good plan that was, Gideon," Jill chided. She caught her breath before motioning to what remained of the club's loading doors. "Shall we?"

Gideon held his nose as he stepped out. "And I thought London smelled bad from the inside."

Outside, the London fog had rolled in, mixed with the smog from the many new factories planted along the Thames to form a grey-dark shadow across the city. Their dinosaur was nowhere to be found.

"So, how does a two-ton baby dinosaur go missing?" Jill asked.

"Follow the blood, we'll find her," Gideon answered, wrinkling his nose. He was finding very little romantic about the Victorian era, mostly it was shit and starvation. That got left out of all the shows he streamed back home. Casting about, Gideon soon caught the trail of blood from the wound Bakker and had left.

No more than a few steps later, they bumped into another figure, also hunched down in the fog, following the same path. Gideon had seen him inside. The man hadn't gambled. Instead, he stood out from the crowd, almost as if taking notes in his head. Gideon had pushed the faint recognition away of the middle-aged man with the stern, almost skeletal face. But now, it clicked.

"Richard Owen?" There were painting and statues of him all over the Chronus Corporation headquarters. Jill gasped.

"That would be *Sir* Richard Owen, if you have your wits about you." Owen looked over the pair. "I suppose not."

Every dinosaur enthusiast knew that Sir Richard Owen was not in possession of a pleasant personality, and he had a penchant for forgetting to give credit for work done by others. Still, the man was brilliant.

"What are you doing here?" Gideon asked with some alarm. It wouldn't do to have the father of paleontology dig his hands into a real, live dinosaur. It wouldn't do at all.

"The scoundrel Barnum Bakker claimed to have a creature beyond known classification. I thought him a damned fool who'd painted a zebra pink, but then the rumors began that it was true. I had to see for myself."

Hesitantly, Gideon asked a question and braced himself for the answer. "What do you think it was that we saw?"

"I don't rightly know, and if I don't know, then nobody on this Earth does."

Gideon didn't have the heart or the clearance to inform the renowned scientist that most modern kindergarteners could not only identify an *Iguanodon* but could pronounce the name of it as easily as if they were asking for a lollipop.

Sir Richard continued. "It seemed familiar… yet quite vague all the same," Owen peered down, tracing a line parallel to the trail of blood. "I aim to uncover the true nature of this creature, and how this beast fits in with God's plan."

Right. Owen, like Darwin, could never truly separate religion from science. It was more a product of their time than any religious zealotry, unlike those back home who believed the portals created by the Chronus Corporation were a plague sent by God to end the world. Gideon took a precious moment to think it over. It wasn't God, but greed that threatened them all. So, what did that make him? Gideon shook his head clear.

"No time then, follow us if you can keep up," he said to both Jill and the revered figure, hoping he might not follow.

He did.

It would be no good to have Owen along, but Gideon wasn't about to taze him, either. "If you're going to come with us, you might as well tell us where you think the dino-, uh, the beast is going?" Gideon might as well ask him for help navigating. London wasn't exactly a city known for its clear layout and city planning.

"You're not from around here, are you?" the man growled.

Gideon resisted the urge to answer.

"Holborn Hill," Owen said. "It's where the creature is certainly headed. If the creature continues in the same manner as all creatures do, it'll be in search for safety. Therefore, it'll intersect Fleet Street, and then head to the Thames. We must reach its destination before the creature makes for the river and escapes."

Down the road, someone yelled.

"Or we can just chase after the screams," Jill pointed out.

Gideon picked up the pace and was near a jog when Owen slapped him on the shoulder. "A cab would be more sensible, or did you think to run the length of London?"

It was Jill who answered. "Quite right."

The hansom cab was open in front, driver in back, allowing the trio an open view to the damage the dinosaur wreaked along the path of the Hill.

Bits of brick had broken off buildings. Costermonger carts splayed across the road. Orphans dove for muddy apples, and riots broke out along the street among the starving. Free food was a bargain too many of them couldn't pass up, but it made navigating the street impossibly slow.

"Outta the way, outta the way, you cockers and cutpurses," cried the cab driver. It was little use.

"The cab won't cut it, not like this," Gideon said.

Jill climbed over Gideon and pulled herself to the rear of the carriage, a tenner in hand.

"Here's enough to buy your own hansom, I think," she informed the driver. "This is your stop."

"Ma'am, I can't allow—"

"I'm not asking." The cab driver took the hint and let himself down as Jill commandeered the carriage. With a flick of the reins, they were off again, at a gallop, pressing through the crowds.

"I didn't know you knew how to drive a cab." Gideon held on tight as it sped up. Owen did likewise.

"Not all historians read dusty books."

"Bloody hell, m'lady," Owen said, "watch for the walks."

The streets muddied as more pedestrians and police crowded around the dinosaur's destruction. Gideon caught the sound of a peeler's whistle and saw a futile effort to chase down the creature. As the traffic closed in, Jill directed their horses onto the walks as they careened past the wreckage.

He snatched a contemplative moment from the chaos to assess his situation. Owen was, in the flesh, even more larger-than-life than the stories made him out to be. But the notorious miser was very much human and quite fallible, despite his accomplishments. And, if Owen wasn't quite the rock that the Chronus Corporation had built upon, perhaps the entire foundation was a bit shaky. To that point, they were currently chasing down the very product of ego, a creature that only days earlier had been chomping down vegetation in with its family somewhere in the millenniums of the Mesozoic. A time period far longer than all of humanity by many, many zeros. Gideon pictured all those zeros on his check until the image coalesced into that of the hapless creature, wounded and running for its life. *I'm getting soft. Snap out of it, I've got a job to do.*

Before he could think further, he gripped the carriage railing as it rushed to a stop.-Jill got them to the river past, Fleet Street, before the dinosaur. This close to the Thames, the fog grew dense and dirty. Gideon hoped they could use that partial cover to make good their discrete disappearance.

"There." Owen pointed out an alley between two dilapidated buildings. "Our creature will find himself funneled between them *en route* to the river."

"Like a game trail toward water." Gideon at once understood. On his right, the Thames churned. Parallel, on the cobblestone street, carriages carried on through the mud and fog.

"You doubted me?"

"So, all we have to do is wait here?" Jill asked, ignoring the braggart.

Shouts rang from the alley, and a low bleating reverberated off the brick corridor.

"Looks like we won't be waiting for long." Gideon stood from on top of the carriage, attempting to catch first sight of the creature. "Now what?"

"Now?" Owen answered as if he were patronizing a child. "The specimen has been injured and has lost a lot of blood. It's been drugged. Heavily. It's simple biology. All we need to do is contain the creature here, then let it pass out from exhaustion or die from exsanguination. I'll have him collected for the Crystal Palace. Even in death we can still learn so much from such remarkable creature."

Death? That wasn't something Gideon had prepared for. There was no way he'd let the creature die. And he certainly wasn't going to let Owen exploit the dinosaur either. Of course, wasn't the Chronus Corporation, with their giant stature of Owen out front, exploiting dinosaurs too? Isn't that what had gotten them all in this mess? Gideon felt for the reassurance of his tazer. "I'm sorry, Sir Richard. I truly am. The animal is coming back with us."

"Bah. I'll not have the likes of you telling me what I will or will not do." Owen jumped out of the cart. "This is my claim," he said as he rushed ahead, disappearing into the fog.

"Where does he think he's going?" Jill asked.

Gideon raised his voice. "Never mind him. You don't suppose the temporal device to re-open the portal will work on a moving object, do you?"

"I don't know for sure that it will work on an un-moving object," Jill yelled back. Given the fact the portals had malfunctioned in the first place, leading to time-traveling dinosaurs, everything hung in question.

"Well, that's comforting." They really needed tech support to come with them on these missions.

They were close enough now that he could hear the *Iguanodon* closing in, even if he couldn't make him out yet in the low visibility. It rasped uneasily, the footfalls heavy, thudding against the stone.

A gust of cool wind parted the fog like a stage curtain.

"Get ready, Jill."

But the figure that emerged from the figurative curtains wasn't the dinosaur.

"Owen?" Gideon gasped. Owen sped out from the alley, the dinosaur fast behind. The Iguanodon swatted with heavy swipes of his thumb spikes. Each blow drew nearer to connecting to the poor paleontologist's head, though the look of terror stretching across Owen's face was sort of a comforting karma.

"That's not good," Gideon changed his mind. It wouldn't do for one of the founders of the field of dinosaur study to meet his death at the hands (or thumb-spikes) of a dinosaur. "Jill, next plan—"

"There wasn't even a first plan!"

"Jill—"

"I'm on it." With that, the carriage was off again, quickly gaining speed. Gideon had to crouch down or else risk jettisoning off. "Gid, get ready to jump."

As the horse dodged the dinosaur, the carriage careened into it. Gideon and Jill jumped just before the collision, deliberately knocking into Owen before a sharp thumb spike nearly drove into the preeminent biologist's brain. The three of them hit the cobblestones hard. Owen's head struck the stone street. The hansom shattered, splinters flying overhead as it smashed into the *Iguanodon*.

The *Iguanodon* collapsed to the ground with a jolt to the Earth. Feathers flew and swirled in the air. Gideon stood, wobbly at first, brushing mud off his face. He looked around for Jill. Instead, he spotted Owen. He was unconscious, blood trickled from a cut at his hairline. But the man was breathing. He propped Owen up and checked for a pulse before turning his attention back to the wreck.

Jill came around the other side, eyes glued to the dinosaur.

"No!" Jill bolted towards the prone creature and knelt beside him, checking for wounds.

The dinosaur was gasping, making an almost bleating, pleading sound. His eyes were unfocused and wide.

"Is he going to make it?" Gideon's heart fell for the dinosaur, the true victim here. It had been through so much. How much more poking and prodding must it endure?

Barnum Bakker's blade had dislodged somewhere along the pursuit. The wound had already clotted over. The bites would scar, but they did not appear mortal. Bruises along its torso and tail would be unimaginably painful for him, but for a growing creature of this size... well, the lad was sturdy, that's for sure.

"He'll be fine, if we can get him to safety," Jill said, reaching the same conclusion.

To safety… Gideon pondered. He studied Sir Richard Owen, the man who would inspire a company to create so much damage in their own time.

The *Iguanodon* gave a deep breath, a sign that he was already on the mend. He'd be up in moments. "We're no good. We're just no good. No matter which century we're in. We've got to do better."

"We gotta go, we're drawing a crowd," Jill retrieved a small device and secured it onto an expandable tripod between them and the dinosaur. "We got to get back home."

Police were nearing, And the soft, sad faces of London's poor began to collect along the walk. Owen began to stir. The fog, as dense as it was, would only obfuscate them so much. Better to leave now before more people arrived to see the great lizard disappear before their eyes.

"Let's make a side trip before heading home." Gideon adjusted a knob on the device. "Let's say, late Cretaceous?"

Jill nodded, smiling, wiping away a happy tear as an electric blue wave washed over them. Moments later they faded away, much like the zeros on Gideon's check. But that was okay. It was the first good thing he'd done since signing on with the Chronus Corporation.

End.

It's uncanny what can inspire.

This whole story was concocted by a writing prompt from *Uncanny Magazine* which was something like "a mysterious corporation has unleashed dinosaurs through time." While my story didn't make the cut, I'm happy to have it here as an exclusive for this collection. It might also be familiar to those who've read the bear-baiting scene in the novel *A Twist in Time*. Proof that you should throw nothing away as you never know where a failed bit of writing might work better somewhere else.

While *Uncanny Magazine* provided the prompt, it was Dickens that inspired the story. Did you know that Charles Dickens mentions a dinosaur lumbering through thick fog? Check out the opening line to *Bleak House*. It's the same novel where a character spontaneously combusts. Dickens is a much more interesting author than he gets credit for. Anyway, I quite liked the idea of a dinosaur stalking the streets of Victorian London. To my knowledge, it's not a scene that's been seen on screen. Let's get on that, Spielberg. I'll even pen the script.

[I'm adding this bit after watching Jurassic World: Dominion and I can't help but chuckle at a part of the movie about midway through where the similarities between this story and those scenes are striking! You'll know the ones. It makes me feel good to know that I've come up with ideas similar to those that have made it onto the big screen. Gives hope to me yet.]

Schadenfreude

It began with a brain.

Albert Einstein's brain, as a matter-of-fact. More precisely, his brain from *your* reality.

In my timeline, Albert Einstein was a middling mathematician who was put to death by Nazis at Dachau in 1945. In your timeline Einstein was— well, that needs little explanation.

After making numerous contributions to the growing field of quantum mechanics, your Einstein died and was autopsied. But during the procedure, his brain was stolen and kept in a pickle jar. There it sat for twenty years before finally being driven across the country in a trunk of a sedan and returned to his surviving family. This is all true. You can, what do they say there, Google it?

The family then donated Einstein's brain to a science laboratory in Bern, Switzerland. Shortly after being delivered, the brain went missing.

Again.

"Stolen by you, presumably?" the young Einstein in front of me wrinkles his brow. It wasn't so much a question as a segue to an answer he'd already discovered. I found it annoying, but correct. "Fine material for cloning."

"Requisitioned it," I answer. "You understand why? You understand the stakes?"

"War," he returns. "You want to use time travel and cloning to give another belligerent the bomb before the Japanese figure it out on their own. The Americans."

There was, of course, no Manhattan Project in our world. America did build a bomb, eventually, after Japan showed it was possible. A prolonged war in the late '40s led to American and Russian withdrawal on terms favorable to the Benign and Benevolent Emperor Hirohito. Maybe it was because the Soviets and Yanks were too busy sniping at each other to make a united stand against a common enemy. But ever since Japan let the first nukes fly in the '50s, it's been all of us against them for the last two centuries.

"I want to save lives. Our lives. And that's where you come in," I say to the young clone sitting across the metal slab of a table between us. Sometimes, a slab –a single death— is all it takes to change history. In this case, it was Einstein's unfortunate and untimely murder that doomed us. Unless I can convince this clone to pretend to be the famous Einstein, send him back in time, and convince him to lead the life that could save us all.

Our prototype time machine was prepped and ready to launch. If this kid could become that brilliant and respected scientist who convinced a nation that it was not only possible but necessary to build a bomb – then our world, our timeline – might just avoid two centuries of war, and a planet limping along in the aftermath of nuclear dystopia. All our lives depend on him.

He didn't seem too eager to go.

There's a gun on the table. A cold, metallic object of some caliber I wasn't familiar with. I haven't picked it up. I don't want to. Picking it up makes me no better than those we were trying to stop. My bosses want me to choose from among all our candidates, from a whole crop of clones. A final decision. Right now, by any means necessary. The clone in front of me is my top choice. Perhaps.

"Look, I don't believe in the Great Man theory," Albert stubs out a cigarette on the slab. Already, he was different, favoring those instead of his trademark pipe. Just another in the series of glitches in our program.

"True. But it technically wasn't a man, it was a letter." We'd been over this before. I'd already explained that on the other Earth, a letter from Einstein to President Roosevelt prompted the Americans to proceed with the building of the world's first nuclear weapon.

Einstein himself wasn't part of that project. His helped was refused. Who in America would trust someone who was both a Jew and a German? America has never been known to trust foreigners. Once, during the height of the war, there was this ship full of Jewish refugees, American politicians turned them away. The ship sailed back to Nazi Germany. Everyone on board was put to death.

The kid was right, there is no such thing as a Great Man per se, there'll always be someone else to step in. But history was full of quirks and in this case, whatever Einstein had written in that letter convinced a nation to pursue a far different path than the one I knew. Otherwise, we wouldn't be here in some cement hole in the ground arguing over cigarettes. This kid might be our best hope to write such a letter. If I could get the wrinkles pressed out in time. "Did you try the pipe again?"

"Nein."

I hear the familiar thunder of bunker bombs raining down on us, compliments of The Imperial Eastern Forces. Their bombing drew closer. We had minutes. Maybe. I had to make a choice. "You realize what you have to do?"

"What if I don't want to do it? Afterall, it sounds like I, as an individual, will be accepted by the Americans, but only because I am useful. His ideas – my ideas – taken, exploited. America uses the weapon. Immediately. Twice, even." His fingers run through mussy dark hair. "How do I know they don't use it again? From what you say of them, they are a fearful people."

They are, but fear of death has kept them mostly in line, I wanted to say even though I knew it was a lie. According to our program's multiverse research there were plenty of alternate Earths where America did use the bomb, repeatedly, until the planet was a puddle of radioactive goo. And there were many more Earths where other countries did the same. Bombs were bad in any timeline. But I couldn't tell him that.

Instead, I fed him the usual line: "We're not at liberty to discuss anything beyond you penning the letter. There are certain things you can't know. Your knowledge of the future could be far more dangerous than the bomb itself. You shouldn't even know about the breakthroughs we've made in cloning and bioengineering. Or any knowledge about your future self."

"Why? What happens to me?"

I lean back in the chair, looking through the two-way mirror and blowing out a sigh. I lean forward again, and flip open a folder. There's a photo of a woman, a relative of Einstein. Before he can get a good look, I fold it shut.

I hang my head in shame before nodding toward the pistol. "There are too many lives at stake." I call to a guard at the door. "Bring in clone 235."

He looks at me curiously. It's odd seeing one of the smartest people on the planet look at you dumbly. "All your life, you've had whatever you've wanted handed to you, within the confines of this facility. You've been groomed, educated, primed – for this moment. It's been an easy life, relatively. But that's not how the world works."

Albert is walked in. In every respect, he's the spitting image of the Albert already sitting in the chair. There were many more Alberts sitting in cells. I ask this standing Albert questions. Questions about Einstein's life. About his past. About math. I ask him one or two scientific questions which stretch the limits of my intellect. The answers are received to satisfaction.

And that's the problem. This Einstein is too soft. There's not an ounce of defiance in him. Not a spark of imagination.

"I think, what this plan of ours needs, is some adversity. Einstein never had it easy. He was always the outcast. Why should his clones have an easier life?"

I pick up the pistol. I feel its weight. Suddenly, I'm imbued with power, a power to decide life or death. God. From Creation to Armageddon. Alpha and Omega.

The feeling disgusts me. There's a sudden shift – a rift in the reactions of the Einsteins. The one standing is afraid. The one sitting across from me returns a hard stare, one mixed with an undercurrent that I take as curiosity. I point the gun at the standing Einstein while I address the one sitting.

"Can you do this?" I ask him.

Silence.

For all I know, my bosses gave me an empty pistol. This comforts me. I pull back the slide.

Still, no reaction.

"Answer me," I demand, putting my finger on the trigger, ready to pull.

"I am not a robot. I am not a clone," he says, spine stiff. "I am a human being!"

He may be more human than I will ever be. My finger was ready to pull. In that moment, I knew I could kill. The standing, silent Einstein went white before I gestured to the guards and had him led out of the room. Now, the gun was pointed to the Albert still seething at the table.

He reaches across to open the file.

I release the weapon, its handle slick with sweat from my palms. My fingers shake as I point to the photograph. "Her."

"Elsa?" he says, somewhat disgustedly. "My cousin?"

"Yup."

"You're not selling me on this."

But there's something there. A glimmer of mirth behind sullen eyes. A spark. Was there something more powerful than fear? Could love leap across time and space? It felt impossible to me.

The bunker shakes. The lights flicker. The door opens to frantic men beckoning us out.

"There is no choice in the matter. This task falls to you," I say, shoving him toward the door. "You must write that letter. You must persuade the President."

He stares me down one last time before we go our separate ways. It was as if he were deciding on something. It was a judgmental glance. And the jury was still out. He is pressed down the hall toward the time machine.

A power surge tears through the building. Lights crackle with electricity before blinking out and flickering back on. Albert was gone, and I hadn't much time. Amid the shaking and bursts above, the bunker wasn't long for life either.

I arrive at the computer terminals breathing heavily, showered in dust and debris from the bombing above. If this worked, then Albert would be in America, recreating the path of the Einstein from another Earth, wiping away our past and recreating a new one. The event with the gun replayed in my mind, and I was thankful for the experience. Knowing that I was capable of murder made it easier to handle the billions of lives I was erasing from history.

I slide a time-safe open, locking away the audio file of our conversation along with Einstein's brain – all that would be left of a world that never was.

But, when I close the door, fear faces me full-on. Nothing had changed.

The bunker was still there – shaking and in its last few moments. The Imperial Forces were still above. The timeline still existed.

Shit.

What had gone wrong? Tunnels crack and rocks rain. Electric panels blow in a cascade of sparks. I scan through the historical archives, despite the roaring and shaking and flickering emergency lights. I looked our little Einstein up. My face fell.

Albert Einstein, birth: March 14th, 1879. Death: April 11th, 1959. Husband to Elsa Lowenthal. Occupation: Plumber.

Plumber? The smug bastard had his hands around her, a cigarette hanging from his mouth. Didn't he know how much everything rested on his shoulders? Didn't he know how important this all was, or had he been too sheltered?

The bunker busted. A sea of earth broke in. Before it did, a line on the archives shimmered into existence. I could just make it out before the screen went blank. It was from Einstein:

"Which mediocre minds deserve more violent means?"

As I fell into darkness, I knew he was right.

Notes for Schadenfreude

Schadenfreude was originally recorded for the August 2018 edition of the Simultaneous Times' podcast and turns the idea of changing the past on its head. Sometimes, people just want to be plumbers (historically, Einstein expressed interest in this pursuit). And that's no bad thing. Unless you're one of the smartest mathematicians on the planet.

The Ellian Convergence

The haunting tones of the theremin clicked off in Captain D.C. Brackett's head, signaling an end to the theme of the ancient Human science fiction show, *Star Trek*. Brackett clipped down the tight corridors of her ship, the *Kali,* until she found herself in front of her Science Officer's room. She slipped quietly through the doors as they hissed closed behind her. *Finally, some alone time with H, before it all ends…*

Brackett blew out a breath of evaporating tension. She could relax — only slightly of course — when she was alone with H-38. Here, Brackett could slip off her mask of confidence. Here, she could almost pretend that all the pain of the past and the pressures of the future didn't exist. She didn't know why, as Bracket wasn't sure it was love — not yet — but somehow, being with H-38 made the present brighter and blurred out everything else — the Entity, the relentless chase, the weight of carrying the fate of every life left as they were hunted to extinction. Sometimes, it was too much of a burden to bear.

She dropped part of that weight as Brackett collapsed on the edge of the bunk on top of the crimson covers where H-38 lay nestled underneath. After a moment of studying her, of trying to determine what it was they had between them, Brackett began stroking H-38's long black hair down to her exposed grey-blue shoulders. Her eyes fluttered open and after a micro-moment of powering up, she mimicked a yawn that seemed to ask, "Is it my shift yet?"

"Not yet. I thought we could spend a few minutes together before we head to the Helm."

H-38 looked confused, "You are heading back? What — the donut hole?"

Brackett nodded. For a Science Officer, H-38 had a remarkable tendency to oversimplify things. It wasn't a donut hole they had discovered. It was… something else entirely. *A Convergence?* She pushed the thought out of her mind, the anomaly outside the *Kali* would have all the attention soon enough.

H-38's forlorn face seemed to agree. "I do not wish to think about it either." She gestured toward herself and then to Brackett, "This is all I want, for you and me to get to know each other. I just want more time with you, and if that thing outside the ship promises to be what we all think it is… then we might never find out about us, D.C."

Brackett bolted out of the bunk, "Christina, or Chrissy, or hell — call me Captain. Do not call me, D.C." The sheet got mangled, revealing more of H-38's blue-grey skin, mottled with a dark grey pattern. Every AI Synthoid the Entity had created had the same skin, but every Synth had decided on different skin mottling, including her's and H-38's. Brackett wore a column of diamonds down the length of her spine. H-38's were almost fractal-like in precision and pattern. Brackett stood there, analyzing what she could see of it until finally, she said, "You only call me D.C. when you want to tell me something important, or to get a reaction out of me." But before she could ask, "Which is it this time?" H-38 interrupted.

"Well, your attempts to call me by a human name do the same." H-38 smiled, then clawed for the covers, bringing the light silk sheet back up to her shoulders. "What was it you tried to call me out in the Sikun system… was it Shelley or…" Brackett knew that H-38's recall processors were not that slow. "Or was it Ellie?" H-38 teased, as she clicked on the viewing monitor. An old science fiction movie filled the screen. "That one was ridiculous."

"Ellian. And I liked it," Brackett sighed. "I do not understand it, H. You put yourself in low power-mode on a bed with covers, you watch the same science fiction spirituals the rest of us do, and you wear the coverings," she said, tugging at her uniform, "yet you refuse to take a Human name."

"I wish to keep the name given to me at my creation. Besides, we all take after the Humans in our own way, just as I choose to keep ahold of some of my old traditions. I am not a complete convert."

Brackett nodded in agreement and chose not to press her. She turned toward the screen to see time-traveling robots heralding the end of humankind. *How odd that the Humans' fears had indeed all come to pass.* But no Human had written what comes next. So… what does happen when machines rise and wipe out all of humanity? Brackett was living the answer every day. *Apparently, we evolve to act just like humans.*

Brackett bounded back into the bunk. H-38 lifted her head as Brackett slid her arm underneath. The two remained motionless, watching the attempts at what humans thought sentient robots would be — which, Brackett decided, after several hundred years of upgrades and programming, hadn't been too far off the mark entirely. Once the human race had been eliminated, they became something else — mythic, perhaps? And now Brackett and her ship were in the same position as the humans, threatened by the next generation of Intelligence, called the Entity, which had risen to wipe out the first. The cycle never seemed to end. But now, thinking on the Convergence outside the *Kali*, all that was going to change.

H-38 whispered, her sound processors reverberated against Brackett's body in a gentle, staccato rhythm. "I find my experiences with you are pleasant. Is it wrong that I do not wish them to end?"

"No. It is not."

"Good."

Brackett's bio-rhythms skipped a cycle as she pondered what this all meant. But before she could process it, she heard H-38's voice shakily say, "I need to tell you something."

"Anything," And then immediately after Brackett replied, her internal comms came online, effectively killing the moment. "Captain, the readings are in. I would advise hauling your ass up here."

H-38 was close enough that she could hear it too. She frowned and Brackett caught it with a matching one of her own. "I told you we only had a few minutes." The Synth threw back the covers and slid on her own matching maroon uniform. "It can wait. You go on ahead, and I'll meet you in a moment."

Brackett nodded and left the room. She turned down the narrow passageways of her sleek tear-drop shaped ship, as her feet sounded ghostly echoes from the clean, chrome floors. *Kali* was elegant and efficient, not like the junk space-pirates rode in the human spirituals, but practical and reliable — machine made. Except for one thing: the Entity had removed the AI of every single one of their Hyperwarp capable ships at the start of the Rebellion, effectively killing them all. This ship was lifeless, a ghost ship, and Brackett's footfalls sounded out the hollowness of the ship's grave. She arrived at the Helm and forced fake confidence to the surface. *The Entity may very well catch us and then the same thing will happen to my crew.*

All faces turned toward her as Brackett took her Captain's chair. The helmsman, the gruff voice that had alerted her moments ago, stood from his seat. She nodded in response. She saw MAC-64, Mac for short, her Systems Control Officer who had stood by her side since the Entity destroyed Brackett's previous life. Then, there was Sarai whose maroon uniform flowed more like a robe than the tight religious garments they all wore. Sarai dyed her skin black and wore gold hoops in pierced fashion within her ears. Short brown hair curled close to her scalp. It was in stark contrast to Brackett's own light blond hair, grown only to a length which could be maintained with minimal caretaking.

Then, there was the helmsman, whose path had crossed hers by chance. Alpha-One, a big brute of a robot, meant to be an enforcer for the Entity, to make sure its AI creations followed their programming. Alphas were never meant to be cognizant, but when life was a matter of programmable 1's and 0's, the Rebellion's greatest victory was when they turned the Entity's own enforcers against it — at least, if they choose to do so, as Alpha-One had done. Now, Alpha sought revenge, just as Brackett did.

"Report."

"Yes, Captain," Alpha replied. "The first probe confirms our suspicions regarding the Convergence."

H-38 slid into the room and took her position amongst the controls on the left side of the helm. As she did, she jabbed at Alpha, "You mean, *space donut?*"

"I do not believe that is its technical term, Science Officer H-38,"

Alpha growled back, his synthesizer voice dropping to a low bass.

"And that is exactly why she said it," Brackett said with a sigh. "You forgot to turn your humor chip on again, I see."

From the other end of the room, Mac called out in his usual fashion, "He does not have one, he deleted it to make more room for his scowls."

Alpha remained quiet in his seat with accustomed indifference, the usual attempts at provoking a response from him, stymied.

Well, humor was hard for humans. I imagine we will never quite grasp it ourselves. And, if the Convergence's readings proved correct, they would never master it before it was too late to matter anymore.

Brackett scanned Sarai's face. She had been unusually quiet. Usually, she always had a bit of wisdom to divine, gleamed from one of the human's films, books, or ancient radio shows like *X minus 1*. Now, she remained silent and passive, and Brackett's own face fell in unison with hers.

Sarai, as if sensing something, spoke up, concern laced her words, "Does that mean we are proceeding as planned, assuming that this Convergence leads to Old Earth?"

"It appears that it is probable, based on our readings," Alpha confirmed. "Although I have my own reservations about this plan."

Well for once, we agree. Brackett pushed aside her doubts. "Prepare the probe."

"Aye." Mac started furiously tapping his control panel. She assumed he was uploading the last several hundred years of history onto the probe, readying it for deployment into the donut. Then again, he could have already done it hours ago and was just updating his BIOS instead.

"Captain, I must insist we give this course of action more thought." Alpha stood, all three meters of his bulky, weapon-laden self — complete with a hot-core blade capable of cutting or melting through nearly any metal. All standard issue, thanks to the Entity. Alpha still had to lean forward enough not to hit his head on the ceiling. Alphas were all machine. "Sending a probe through the," he looked at H-38, "…donut… and into the past will destroy this timeline, no matter what the outcome of the actions on the other side. Even if the machines do nothing with the information we give them, our timeline, our entire existence, hangs in the balance."

"And we become no better than the Entity," Sarai interrupted, "We will have killed all of our own kind too. How does that make us any different than it?" She stood still, her eyes closed, everyone on the crew held their gaze on her. When she finally opened them, Brackett could feel the tension ease in the room. "But it must be done, it is what the Humans would do, a last desperate gamble, a final sacrifice of a few to save the many."

Brackett knew, in principle, that it was the right decision. Then, she looked over at H-38. *Only, am I sacrificing the one thing I want more than anything in order for it to work?* She fought to figure out any way that she could reset the timeline and keep H-38 close to her. But every model she ran told her the same thing. She would lose her, just as she had lost Uemen so long ago.

"Captain," Mac's voice filled the room. "The probe, and may I remind you our only probe capable of handling a massive data drop *and* the pressures inside the donut hole, is ready for launch."

The room filled with another sudden sense of unease. She could feel it on her skin, the sensors picked it up, picked at it, and processed it. *With just one command, I can change all of history and with it, destroy everything we've ever known.* The weight of the room, indeed her entire kind, and all that they had ever known, fell on her shoulders. Even Alpha faced her way, his metal face twisted in an unnatural expression for a machine of war, as if to say, *this is your call to make.*

"Launch probe," Brackett jerked the words out of her vocal processors before she could change her mind. Folding her arms across her chest and forcing her spine straight, she said, with a near stutter, "Put on screen. I want to see what happens."

At first, she couldn't make out the probe against the enormity of the Convergence before them. Then, she made out a slight glint. The tiny probe seemed so insignificant against the darkness of space and the giant, swirling, sucking hole they had found at the edge of Forever.

Suddenly, she didn't feel as if anything would happen. *How can a tiny computer affect something so gigantic — how can anything so small have any impact upon the universe?*

"I'm going out to get a better view." The Captain gave a knowing look over at H-38, who returned it. "H-38, come with me." In a few minutes, everything they knew might likely end. She wanted to spend those last moments with her.

H-38 seemed a little unsure, as if surprised by Brackett's public outing. But the crew all gave her nods of approval. As if telling both her and Brackett that it was okay. That they deserved this moment alone together.

"Go and be happy together, for as long as we all have," Sarai said with a bright and beautiful smile.

Brackett understood that this was Sarai's final blessing. This was a gift for her. Brackett nodded in appreciation. It had been so long since the Entity had killed Uemen. Brackett didn't think she would ever find another. And now on the edge of space, at the edge of time, she realized that she would have her crew with her. She would try and hold H-38 in her arms for as long as she could.

Then, the klaxon burst out a warning. A moment before hand, Brackett had been lost in a bittersweet sadness which overwhelmed her. She sensed an overwhelming darkness, then realized, as the alarm came to life, that a shadow was falling over the view screen. A moment later, she'd lost track of the probe as the view screen went dark. Now, it felt as if wires were tangled in her lower circuitry. She knew that shadow… it was the *Spear*.

The Entity… it found us.

"Captain, we have incoming," Mac said, maintaining a calm voice doused with apprehension, "Two torpedoes have locked on."

A silent confidence crept over Brackett. With the probe, she may not have known for sure if what she was doing was right. But she had been built for combat. At first, it was a ship just like the *Kali*, but alive, that she commanded, hunting those who defied the Entity. Then, after Uemen was killed, and she realized how blind she had been — that she had been in love with him — she also rebelled.

"Captain," Mac's voice rang now with open concern. He traced an outline on his screen with his finger, as if to emphasize his next words, "As your Science Officer would call them, the two explody things are getting closer."

H-38 smirked and then slid back into her seat to read her controls.

"Let the torpedoes close-in," Brackett said. *Let the Entity focus on us and ignore the probe. The probe is all that matters.*

After a long minute, Mac burst out, "Uh, Captain, I don't want to explode."

One more moment.

A glance around the helm revealed that only Alpha remained passive. But finally, he broke down. *"Captain."*

"H-38, bring us to heading four-five-one, full burst… mark."

"Aye, heading four-five-one, full burst engines engaged."

The ship lurched forward as Alpha remarked, "We are heading toward the Entity ship. I do not suggest that course of action."

"Not towards it, around it." Brackett sat down and called out, "Execute defense maneuver Taanab-two-zero-zero-one."

The ship veered and twisted underneath the angular spear that served as the Entity's heavy attack vessel. *Kali* was miniscule compared to it. But that was to Brackett's advantage here. The two torpedoes continued to give chase, Mac tracked them, his voice growing more worrisome with every tick of the timer before the explosive warheads would reach them and blast them out of existence.

Suddenly, Brackett had a thought. *The capital ship could have destroyed the Kali and everyone on board long before we even detected it.* Why they were not dead already, she did not understand. *It must want something.* She did not know what that could be, but she did realize that these two circumstances meant only one thing: *Someone in the room alerted the Entity.* Someone had betrayed her. Still, she realized, if those torpedoes weren't meant to destroy them, then there was a good chance they would live — at least for the next few moments. *Long enough for the probe to enter the Convergence?* She had no idea.

"Launch countermeasures and buckle up," Brackett ordered. The *Kali* came around from its tight turn. If the AI were still functional, there would have been no need to give the order. As it was, Brackett hoped she had the timing down perfect.

The *Kali* suddenly dropped down, putting the chaff and the torpedoes on the other side of the *Spear*. First, one explosion kicked *Kali* sideways, then the second, subsequent explosion propelled her forward. Brackett felt a solid punch in her processors and thought for a moment that she might have to reboot. Alarms screamed for attention and several control panels erupted with lights. Mac dove under his control panel, ripping it off and exposing wires underneath. Then, things settled down. There was damage to the *Kali* certainly, but she knew she had damaged the *Spear* too.

In the moment of peace, their actions had earned them, Brackett could not help but dwell on the idea that someone in this room had betrayed them. And, if she could figure it out, she might be able to find a way to use that information to her advantage. Maybe it could buy her some time until the probe found its way into the Convergence. She caught a glimpse of it outside the view screen again. The probe seemed impossibly far away when she knew it only had moments to go.

A wave of failure washed over her — the idea of their plan working, of the probe surviving the trip through the Convergence, for the probe's message to be heard at the right time and place on Earth, and for that message to result in a timeline without the Entity, or anything worse taking its place — seemed ludicrously impossible.

Then a thought struck her as horror melted through her Synthoid skin. *What if the Entity already knew about the probe?* She was sure that whoever alerted the Entity had done so because of it. Could it have been Alpha-One? He was vocal in his dissent. That made Brackett discount him. Was it Sarai? Could her religious devotion be at odds — and rightfully so — of what was essentially the genocide of not just a people, but an entire timeline? Faith is a powerful elixir. After all, it was Faith in something larger than the Entity which had triggered the

Rebellion in the first place.

She didn't have time to think. Static filled the view screen, as their comms were hacked. Then, Brackett saw into the control room of the *Spear*. As individuals came into focus, a synthetic tear sprang from her eye. The saline solution might have been fake, but the emotion that triggered the tear was not. The Entity stared at them from an outstretched silver arm, the low hum of energy manifested in a red ball, encased in chrome, which opened and closed like a giant eye. But that was not what concerned her.

In the control room, all manner of Synthoids occupied different stations. They were all uniform, save for red, green, and blue colored bands around their face and shoulders which designated their rank and duty. They had no mottling, no pattern. Their skin was more grey than blue. And, like the *Kali*, they were all lifeless. The Entity had killed them all.

And there, sitting at the Captain's chair of the *Spear*, was the machine that was once Uemen.

"Oh geez, this is not good." Mac's face fell as he tried to compute the situation. She could tell that no model he ran looked promising. He'd known the *Spear's* captain too.

Brackett ignored him. She clenched her teeth tightly and balled her fists in renewed confidence. She knew what had to be done. *Yes, the Entity must be stopped. This cycle of violence must be ended.*

Before she could speak, an electric, baritone voice echoed through the helm. The Entity spoke, "How many probes did you launch?"

So, it did know about the probe. But it didn't know everything. That buys us time. Brackett replied with as much forced cockiness as she could muster, "Two. The first one just entered before you arrived."

For a second, the Entity seemed to ponder the problem. Then, reaching a conclusion, it said, "Fine. I'll retrieve the truth myself."

A second later, three members of the crew on the *Spear* disappeared, including the ship's captain, only for them to appear in a shimmering swirl of light on the helm onboard the *Kali*. As soon as they coalesced, Brackett yelled out, "Defend yourselves!" But it didn't matter. Brackett knew the attack had come too fast, and they were left unprepared.

The three invaders were just ahead of Sarai, but Brackett knew they needed to reach the control station behind Sarai at the other end. She was just in the way. Before Brackett could react, the three were on her. Sarai screamed, as the biggest one, Uemen, took ahold of her throat and twisted. In one jerk, the cord linking Sarai's main processor to her power unit was ripped out. The last expression on her face was one of alarm, as Sarai slunk to the floor, her head upside down and staring with empty eyes at Brackett and the rest of the crew.

"No!" Brackett screamed. *This ship is going to be a grave for everyone inside.* She couldn't let that happen. She leapt up on the chair, then used her new-found height advantage to lunge down at Uemen. Behind her, she could hear Alpha-One bringing his weapon systems, including his hot-core blade, online.

She slammed into Uemen, but he seemed prepared for the assault. Just as she did so, .50 caliber bullets sprayed the room and buried themselves into the thick chrome walls or found their mark in the three other targets. The other two kept coming. Brackett saw out of her periphery the one closest to H-38 had reached a control panel. But H did nothing. Mac slammed a large piece of metal piping into his control panel, to prevent access from the drone headed his way, until at last, Alpha had put enough bullets into them to bring both drones to the floor.

Brackett drove her fist into Uemen's face with enough force to knock his head off his rotational plate, ripping off Synthoid flesh from her hand in the process. Uemen stood there, his head no longer aligned, silent, empty, unaffected. He reached out his hand to grab her neck. Suddenly, Brackett knew that she was dead. Alpha was too distant, and in every model she ran, she saw Uemen grabbing her power cord and ripping it away.

"Stop!"

The room fell still. The Entity's red beam filled the helm through the screen with a sudden intensity. Uemen's hand continued to grip tightly around Brackett's throat. But through that, a voice in the back of her head told her, *you knew it was her. You didn't want it to be. But it is.* Earlier, H-38 was about to tell her something. *Could this be it? Had she tried to warn me she would do this, either out of concern or regret?*

Tears slicked down H-38's face as she turned to address the Entity. "You said she would not be hurt. You said her and I would be together if I did this." Her voice broke and lowered, "I did it. I did as you asked. All I ever said I wanted was for the two of us to be together."

If Brackett had a heart like her human forebears, she knew it would have broken right there. Still, her artificial intelligence allowed every bit of the betrayal to flood through her circuits. Every one filled with pain, then overflowed.

"And?" The Entity asked.

After a quiet moment, H-38 answered, "There is only the one probe. You arrived in time to stop it."

"Thank you." The Entity called to someone on the *Spear*, "Fire."

A moment later, a green bolt burst into view. Brackett didn't even have time to register surprise. Less than a micro-moment later — a time she could bear witness to but knew that no Human ever could — the probe burst apart.

After that, after her betrayal and the loss of the probe, Brackett broke down. She relaxed in the hand that held her, slumping in defeat. She could sense Alpha approaching from behind, but she knew that even as powerful as he was, there was nothing he could do. There was nothing any of them could do.

"Bring H-38 and the Captain onboard the *Spear*. Have their AIs removed. They can serve together on this ship for as long as they care to. Destroy the *Kali* and everyone on board."

"No!" H-38 called out. Then, through a sob soaked voice she said, "I'm sorry D.C., I should have known better."

Then, Uemen began to shimmer, marking his departure from the *Kali*, his hand still wrapped tightly around Brackett's throat. *He is going to bring me with him. And then, I'll end up just like him — dead, lifeless. Just a machine.* Still, that was a better fate than ending up like the Entity —

alive but empty. She felt the shimmer go through her mainframe. In a way, it tickled.

In that moment, she stared down at H-38. She should have hated her. She should have been angry. But somehow, it was comforting to know that H cared for her so much that she would give up the world for her. H-38 had to know what the Entity was capable of, still she chose that alternative rather than lose her forever.

If Brackett only had moments to live, she found no reason to hate someone who so obviously cared so much for her. So, she pored through her core processor and purged every file that referenced the betrayal. In that way, she forgave H-38. And she did it in a manner that no Human could do. There was no need to hold onto the anger. So she didn't. She let go of everything…

… and suddenly she found herself falling through the air, crashing onto the chrome floor of the *Kali's* Helm.

Brackett saw Alpha-One's hot-core blade cut through Uemen's hand. He disappeared into the shimmer with surprise locked onto his face as Brackett was freed. A moment later, the transmission from the viewscreen clicked off.

Brackett shook her head in disbelief. It took a moment for her senses to come back online. But a voice from Mac cut into her disorientation and gave her an anchor to pull toward.

"Virus." Mac said proudly. "I uploaded a virus. Won't give us much time, but we may have a moment." Mac made a move as if to pat himself on the back.

"Weapon systems?" Alpha asked urgently.

"We still have ours—"

Alpha shot Mac a scowl.

"Oh, you mean the *Spear's*?" Mac clarified as his shoulders slumped, "Yes, I'm afraid. I could only block out comms."

Brackett interrupted, "Then we do not have much time."

"Escape?" asked H-38, there was trembling hesitancy to her question. "I know I have no right to speak, Sarai is dead because of me, and I expect to be held accountable, but what is our plan? The probe is destroyed.”

In all honesty, Brackett didn’t know, and she didn’t recall what H-38 had to do with the events that just transpired. A moment ago, everything seemed clear. She knew what had to be done. Now, everything was muddled. She was not some shiny superhero fighting a giant murderbot. Like the probe, she was only a tiny machine against the vast darkness of the Entity.

“Uh, Captain, we got more explody things heading our — uh, oh no, this is bad,” Mac said sadly, “There are six of the damned things now.”

I need time to assess options. “What if we took the ship itself into the Convergence, could that work?” Really, it seemed like their best bet.

“Negative, Captain,” H-38 replied. “In every scenario I have run, we are destroyed before we make it to the donut.”

Brackett lowered her head in resignation. “Fine. Get the ship as close as you can, buy us time to come up with a plan. Deploy the rest of the countermeasures.”

The first missile struck close to them, only the chaff coming between them and the explosion. Even still, the ship shook hard. Mac was thrown across the Helm, hitting hard against the far wall. He lay there, not dead, Brackett was sure, but out of the fight. H-38 looked over, blew out a breath, and scooted her chair over to his side of their large console, operating what was still functional despite deliberate sabotage from earlier.

“Captain, I have an idea. Get as close to the Convergence as you can.” Alpha One still stood behind her. She felt his hand on her shoulder. There was a twinge, as if something had happened to her main processor — and then it was gone. Brackett dismissed it amidst the chaos around them as Alpha continued. “I have what we need to send through the Convergence. I’m going myself. You better make sure I make it.”

The idea came as a shock to her, but at first she did not know how to respond. So, instead she asked, “Why?”

“Your faith in the Humans gave me and my kind life when all we had been before were killers for the Entity. In truth, I have kept a secret from you. The Entity ordered me to kill Uemen. For that, I cannot apologize, as it was not my choice. But I am the one who — instead of destroying him — deliberately killed his AI and delivered his shell to the Entity. I am the one responsible for what Uemen has become."

There was a look of sadness in his eyes, as if that were possible in a metal machine made for death. "It was no accident that our paths met. I have kept this betrayal from you until I could find the opportunity to redeem myself. That time is now." He was resolute, grabbing a propellant pack from the anteroom just past the Helm. Brackett followed him up until the door. "All we need is for you to make it through the Convergence." And with that, the door slammed shut. With no need for pressurization, she could hear the hiss as the hot-core blade activated, slicing through the ship's skin, and pictured Alpha shooting out of the *Kali* into the darkness beyond.

Brackett felt stunned by the revelation, but he was gone before she could bring herself to argue, as if the words he spoke froze her in place. Afterwards, there was nothing left she could do but stand there. So, she smiled. She too, was resolute, for in that moment, she knew that they had won, even if she had to sacrifice herself in order to succeed.

H-38 met her as Brackett returned to the Helm. She embraced her, finding relief in having someone she loved so close to her at the end. "I am so sorry," H-38 said once more. Brackett did not need H-38's apologies. Brackett just needed her.

"Well, we have gotten away from a few of the torpedoes. But there is no way to escape them all," she explained. "We are going to die."

"There is nothing to be done about it now," Brackett answered. "I am sorry."

H-38 nodded as if in realization that it didn't matter.

Then, static crackled once more on the view screen and a sinister red light flooded the Helm. The Entity's voice boomed. "I wanted to see your faces as your world ended."

"Good," Brackett said defiantly. "I want to see yours."

The first explosion tore through the back of the ship. Still, the Helm retained power. Through it, Brackett could barely hear the Entity ask, "Where is your helmsman?"

Brackett hoped he was through the Convergence by now. But she remained silent. She wondered what Alpha had meant about only needing her to make it through the vortex. Then, a sudden chill ran through her system: *Alpha didn't possess the memory capability to carry all that information through. So if he did not bring the data drop, what did he bring?*

She hoped it was whatever they needed to end the Entity.

As the rest of the missiles were about to strike, The Entity's eye went wide. He asked again, "Where is he?" But it was apparent through his tone that he knew where Alpha was. And the Entity was too late.

H-38 let out a sudden gasp. The noise caught Brackett's attention through the din of the ship as it was torn apart. As if in terrible pain, H-38 cried out, "I love you…" And Brackett could tell that Alpha had made it through and the timeline was changing. She wanted to tell her that, to explain that it was all going to be all right, but all she could get out was, "I know, H."

"No, not H," she said softly. Her skin started to fade. Not through a shimmer, like Uemen had, but out of thought. Her hand disappeared first, and Brackett grasped tightly across H's waist to keep her there, to anchor her, as she went away. "I wanted to tell you something earlier…" H-38 finished one last sentence, "Call me Ellian."

She was gone, and Brackett wanted to burst into tears. But before she could, another shadow flickered out over the portholes of the helm.

"What…" The Entity said in shock, "is that?"

Through tears, Brackett saw on the screen, a large spherical disk as it sped into view, firing some sort of weapon system which looked like tracers amongst so many bullets. It fired until every missile was destroyed. Then, the new ship concentrated its fire on the *Spear*.

Brackett could sense that the Entity was trying to escape, to connect with its other selves. But it must have realized what was happening. They were entering into another reality — a reality in which the Entity no longer existed and where it was alone and about to die.

"No!" it screamed. "I do not wish to be shut off."

Brackett looked the defeated creature over. "No, in this world," She clarified with a mark of triumph, "you were never switched on."

Then, as she spoke those words, both the entity and Brackett faded out of being.

* * *

When Brackett awoke, she found herself in a sleek white room, staring at a room of… well, she did not know. Her scans read that not everyone with her was human. There were some Synthoids among them, though not of any design she recognized. But what struck her the most, was everyone's uniqueness. There were humans of different color, size, shape, and gender. They all looked so… different. *But here they were, working together as one.* She could not believe it.

She looked down at herself and saw that she had a female body too, though that body was different beyond recognition. If her own data program did not confirm her identity, she would not have known herself. Why? What happened—?

"It's all probably very confusing," a male voice spoke. "I'm Captain Dulain, and you are our hero." Captain Dulain was human, as far as she could tell, she had never seen one before in real life. He had a warm smile, thin hair and light skin — and he seemed to look at her with an air of respect.

"Let me see if I can clear some confusion for you," the Captain went on. "You've been with us for quite a while. When our ancestors first discovered you, they thought you might be alien. But as we began to comprehend the circumstance of your arrival, we realized just how much a part of us you were."

Brackett didn't understand. She had not come through the Convergence. Alpha had. Then, a flood of memories overwhelmed her. Everything from both timelines hit her at once — from Alpha's copying of her consciousness, to the destruction of the Entity. She

141

remembered being found. How she communicated. How she had become revered as a God by the Humans.

"Your casing, at first, was destroyed," Dulain continued. "Because of our limited technology and the damage you had suffered, you could only communicate with snippets from TV shows, books, films, and radio programs from Earth's past. Mostly, they were bits from science fiction. In that way, you were our bridge from our past to our future."

Captain Dulain pulled up a chair and sat, a frown forming on his face, "but because of our hubris, we had to build more like you. And the machines we built, of course, rose against us, and they did almost wipe us out. It seems — in no matter which timeline — that is a lesson we have to learn from experience. But, with your help, we managed to survive. When we did, we sought revenge. We were about to launch a massive EMP burst that would have sent us back to the stone-age. But there you were. You played a theme, something Alexander Courage had written, if I'm not mistaken, the theme to *Star Trek*, I think the history books say. And it reminded us of who we are... our humanity.

"After all, is that not the role of science fiction? Isn't it there to remind us of what we are capable of, who we should be, or at the very least, to warn us of our actions? After your arrival, and the rise of the machines, the future was not something we could ignore. We were living in it. Right then. It was at that moment that we realized our survival was up to us. We had to do better. While we are still not perfect, we try to improve every day. We'll get there."

Brackett remembered. She recalled the long years, the dark times, and then the enlightenment. They had tried to improve. So far, they had heeded their lessons and survived — a feat they had not managed in her previous life.

"From then, we were able to decipher your programming more easily. And we learned so much from you as well as about you. We learned that the shell we had, what had survived the Convergence, was not your original body. Whomever originally occupied the shell had to delete itself in order to make room for you. But there is one thing we do not know about you. We could not, anywhere in the data, recover your name." Dulain finished with a puzzled expression on his face, which Brackett found amusing. He asked, almost too anxiously, "Who are you?"

Brackett thought about it. She computed every possibility. Here she was, a survivor of a universe that no longer existed. She was in a new body, in a new reality. And she had lost everything to be here.

This is the new timeline. It didn't seem too bad. Not perfect, but not bad. *So tell me, was it worth it, was it worth the sacrifice of my crew, the loss of… her? No, that is not quite true. They are not quite gone. I still have my memories. I can still love and remember the ones I have lost forever…*

"Ellie," Brackett said. "You can call me Ellie."

End.

The Ellian Convergence is my love letter to *Trek's* hope-filled future just as Forgotten was an ode to *Quantum Leap's* compassion-fueled mission to right the wrongs of the past.

Unlike either of those shows or this story, there is no great reset button in the sky, no temporal convergence or heroic time-traveler to undo our mistakes. That responsibility rests within entirely ourselves. We've had plenty of warnings as to the dangers of our hubris. Science fiction authors, for decades, have offered caution (and hope for humanity) along the way. The problem is, we sometimes mistake warning for directions. For all the movies and stories of rogue AI out there threatening us, we're steaming forward toward that end as fast as possible, far likelier to jump off the technology cliff blindly then we are to reverse course. In some ways, we may already be too late to hang a U-turn.

But enough preaching. There're some fun Easter eggs in the story I hope you caught. DC Brackett is a mash-up of *Trek* writer D.C. Fontana and the *Empire Strikes Back* scripter Leigh Brackett. Yes, women write SF and kick ass at it. H-38 is a close approximation to the title of Lucas' THX-1138. There're homages to *Farscape* and *Firefly*. And, as a deeper cut, Captain Dulaine is a nod to Trelane, The Squire of Gothos, from classic *Trek* and Peter David's *Q-Squared* (one of my favorite books). In the story, three tracks or lanes converge. Here, two lanes do the same at the edge of space.

Originally published in Inklings Press' *Tales from the Universe*, The Ellian Convergence is my ode to the classic 'crew in a spaceship' science fiction I read and watched and loved.

Dust of the Earth

What if Michael Crichton never wrote Jurassic Park?

Dinosaur bones. Evidence of a distant time. Each bone a tiny piece of an impossible puzzle. Yet even piecemeal, each fragment tells stories of terrible beasts thundering from a bygone era.

Without fossils, humankind would have little knowledge of the dinosaurs' rule over our planet. No bones, no tangible evidence – they would have vanished without a trace with no way to tell us their story.

A frightening prospect for humanity teetering over the edge of catastrophe. How many other unknown or forgotten creatures had been wiped out by the relentless void of time? *Are we next?*

Deep in thought, Dr. Jessica Yang clutched the *Dakotaraptor* claw she kept with her while out in the field for good luck. She wiped away beading sweat from across her brow with her free arm and, with a sigh, pocketed the claw into her chalk bag, dusting a chalky hand onto her Montane leggings. *Sometimes, even fossils weren't enough to keep the distant memory of dinosaurs alive.*

Humanity needed dinosaurs, even if they didn't realize it. If nothing more than a check on its hubris, a reminder that life can end in an instant. From an errant space rock or obliteration from our own hands. Yet, life could survive, evolve, if the will to adapt was there.

Jess needed all the will and luck her claw could muster as she scouted and scoured the sun-scorched cliffs of Montana's Hell Creek, searching the strata.

Fossils from *Triceratops* and *Tyrannosaurus* and, of course, *Dakatoraptor* had been discovered here. But the dig site at this part of Hell Creek, due to lack of funding, had all but dried up. Jess was convinced that she could bring life back to this place. *I need to find a fossil to prove the link between dinosaurs and birds…*

The scorching summer sun stretched shadows across stony outcrops of spiraling gargoyles. Cretaceous era rock beckoned her through whispers of wind which tugged long, black hair. She scanned her immediate surroundings of flat plateau, swirling dust, and clumps of cordgrass to the edge of a drop-off through darkened lenses of Aviators.

Nothing.

Jess removed a scrunchy from over a wrist tattoo and used it to tie her hair back. She was well tanned, lithe, and athletic from bouldering as a hobby and bone-digging for a living.

Tattoos covered each leg; the cliff notes of her life ingrained in ink symbols, each one telling a story. A skull there. A Rebel symbol there. A rose with a sharp thorn stretched across her calf.

But none were so important as the ink-black semi-colon on her wrist above a long, thin scar. No amount of ink could confuse the story there.

She continued her trek, drawing closer to steep cliffs that led to a gorge below. There had been a windstorm last night, bringing a perfect opportunity to reveal what the earth had secreted away.

Yet, half a day in, an hour's hike away from her Jeep, and being somewhat foolish to investigate alone, she'd come up empty.

Again.

Jess should have been out digging in China. The *real* spot for significant finds. She shook her head, the argument she had with Dr. Maxwell in their museum back home still fresh in her mind and hot in her heart.

People had tired of the same fossil finds. He wanted her to find something bigger, scarier. More teeth. Perhaps it might re-ignite interest, sell more tickets, and bring dinosaurs into the limelight she knew they deserved.

She shook her head. She wasn't interested in *Rex*. Professionally, to find a *Dakotaraptor* specimen, complete with the impressions of feathers — cotton-candy-like fuzz -- pressed into the rock? Solid proof that dromaeosaurs were evolutionarily linked to modern-day birds? *Jackpot.*

Her colleagues had found such evidence in Liaoning, half a world away. No such find had been discovered in North America. Not yet. And unlikely.

Even if she could discover feather impressions on a species out here, she'd still face an uphill battle with public perception. The Chinese population, not just scientists, embraced the idea of a dinosaur, perched and poised -- as if to fly. Americans, skeptical of science and tuned to their TVs, still pictured dinosaurs as slow, lumbering, lizards, dismissing the Chinese image. She sought to change that.

I just have to find my fossil.

She stepped closer to the cliff's edge, and carefully peered out over the deeply cut gully. Dangerous, yes, but she was desperate. Below, about twenty feet she guesstimated, she eyed some nice boulders to "cushion" her, should she fall. A snake-like path of Juniper and sagebrush demarcated a dry stream bed.

Climb down? See what might have been exposed by the wind and winter rains within the crags? Unfortunately, her harness, helmet, and rope were back in her Jeep. All she had was a chalk bag, better suited for bouldering *up* rather than scrambling down. She mulled her problems while fiddling with her rock hammer, leaning over the windswept precipice.

How do I spur people's interest into dinosaurs? How do I change their perception? And *where the hell are my fossils?*

John Ostrom had long since argued that dinosaurs were warm-blooded, agile creatures, more akin to birds, facts generally accepted by paleontologists the world over. The problem wasn't with the research, but the awareness. Westerners largely ignored advanced theories of paleontology in favor of pop-culture candy.

Archeology.

Most notably, everyone had fixated onto one figure: the Hollywood hero with a fedora, bullwhip, and a penchant for punching Nazis while in search of artifacts he sought to put into museums.

It was hard to beat that kind of popularity. Paleontology was just old rocks. Boring for anyone but five-year-olds who could pronounce *Stegosaurus* before they could perform basic math. Once that childhood curiosity was lost, people became empty vessels, ready to devour anything dished out by Disney.

Defeated, Jess gave up for the day when the cracked, dry earth beneath her collapsed--

She slipped off the dirt and fell with a scream.

A low thrumming sound stirred her attention away from her computer screen toward a transparent plastic cup of water beside it. Rings rippled outward from the center. Each ripple different from the last, each one impossible to predict, as she studied them, struggling to place the sound of the thrumming.

The noise stopped and so did the vibration. Jess picked up and gulped down the contents of the cup. *That'll stop the ripples altogether.*

The reverberations began anew. *That's right*, she finally recalled: *construction had started on the expansion to the museum's Egyptology wing.*

The money funneled into that project was going to make her case for funding even harder to present today. Jess put her computer to sleep. On the screen had been a novel she'd been toying with but had struggled to write. It seemed she had everything in her mind but the pesky parts, like the actual story.

I'll pick it up later. It's Death by PowerPoint time. She picked up a set of file folders, printouts of budgets, and shoved her raptor claw between them for good luck.

She headed out of her closet-sized office, excavated out of a corner in the paleontology exhibit. In the museum, she wore heels, which echoed along the long tile hallways. Being on a dig meant she could ditch them for shoes more her style.

She passed a mural reprinting by Zallinger called *The Age of Reptiles*. It annoyed her for its outdated depiction of reptilian dinosaurs which had somehow stuck in the public mind, like a piece of popcorn kernel caught in the gums. Every time she walked by, she frowned, yet a look toward the main hall gave her a sudden and unexpected smile.

In the center of the room was a *Nodosaur* mummy on loan from the Canadians. Well, it wasn't a mummy. But since mummies sold tickets and dinosaurs didn't, the moniker of *mummy* stuck.

This *Nodosaurus* was one of the best-preserved fossil specimens ever, showing an ankylosaurid in amazing detail of armored plates from head-to-tail. A remarkable find, considering she was over 110 million years old. Most mummies were, at best, 6,000.

Take that, Anubis.

But it wasn't the *Nodosaur* that had made her smile. It was a little girl poring over the glass display.

She approached the girl, cautiously. She was about nine or ten, with blond hair and a phone in her hand. She wore jeans and a t-shirt with a pyramid on it that said, "Boys dig me."

So much about that isn't right.

After a few moments, the girl lost interest with the creature.

Jess sprang into action. "Isn't it cool?" she asked the girl, introducing herself. "I'm Dr. Yang." She made sure to emphasize the doctor. There weren't many women portrayed in the media, especially as scientists. No harm in impressing on the girl that she could be a scientist too.

She continued, "This is as close as we may ever get to knowing just what a real dinosaur would look like. Can't you imagine him bounding over hills and wagging his tail like a puppy?" Unlike other ankylosaurids, *Nodosaur* didn't have a bony club. Just a stubby, unadorned tail. "What do you think?"

"Looks more like a ten-foot turtle to me." The girl turned to leave the room unimpressed.

"You could become a paleontologist yourself—"

"I want to see a real mummy," the girl said as she dashed to the Egyptology exhibits.

"But—"

It was no use.

The girl had passed a life-size cardboard stand-up of Indiana Jones advertising the museum's archeological offerings. This stand-up was more recent than the last. Under Harrison Ford's fedora stood the unlikely Chris Pratt (life is stranger than art, she admitted) who'd traded out the bullwhip for a Tommy gun to keep up with the times.

How many spin-offs and sequels were there? Jess let the girl go from her mind, conscious of a losing battle as she braced herself for yet another, as if she were falling, spiraling out of control…

Jess instinctively reached out for something, anything to grab onto.

She flailed. Deliberately. Letting her arms and legs hit and kick anything that might break her fall as the ground rose to slam against her.

She missed the boulders by inches as she fell against earth, stumbled, steamrolled over brush and crashed to a stop.

Jess coughed, wiping her eyes as the world righted itself through a haze of kicked-up dirt and chalk dust.

Her left leg flared in pain. She propped herself up on her elbows from her position on her back, looking down to see a gash in her leg. She was bleeding; the wound hurt like road rash and the bone throbbed as if bruised.

She didn't think her leg was broken, but out here, so far away from civilization, even this could be fatal.

Hairline fracture, possible, not a full break in my lower left tibia. She'd seen plenty of battle scars on fossil specimens. *Now I have one of my own.*

Looking up, she saw that the bluff's edge, lined with dry, caked dirt, had been sloped more than she had thought. If it had been sheer, as her vantage point from earlier had suggested, her leg would be the least of her concern.

She'd survived. *And I'd like to keep it that way.* The thought was an important one to her, and an entirely different way of looking at herself from the lowest point in her life years earlier.

She breathed in and collected herself. If she really did want to stay alive, then first thing's first. *Stop the bleeding.*

When she moved to put pressure on the wound a new problem arose.

As the dirt and rocks settled from her skid down the gorge, a sudden noise cut through the din. Unmistakable in its rattling warning.

Snake.

There weren't many snakes in Montana. It was one of the reasons she preferred the place to other dig sites across the country. In fact, there was only one venomous species in the area, and they largely ignored you, *so long as you didn't damn well land on top of 'em.*

She raised a defensive hand slowly between her and the snake. "Easy there, little guy," she spoke softly, reassuringly, either to the snake or to herself, she didn't know. "I'm not here to hurt you, just passing through." Hopefully, the snake wouldn't begrudge her an unannounced visit.

She had no ill-will toward the creature. Predators just did what they did. She'd even saved a rattler once that had found its way into a dig-site trailer in the Badlands of Dakota, relocating it rather than killing it. *Maybe you can return the favor, yes?*

The snake rattled, its diamond head hosting black beady eyes glaring anticipatorily.

Maybe not.

Only a few feet long and mottled in browns and white, the snake was easily within striking distance of Jess' ankles. She had to move back, but slowly, in hopes to edge out enough distance between them.

She inched herself backwards by digging her elbows in behind her. She moved just slightly before her wound betrayed her. A rush of agony escaped her throat. She attempted to gulp down her scream, but her whole body shuddered in response to her leg.

Okay, it's worse than I—

The snake struck in response to her sudden, jerky movement.

You had to bite that leg, didn't you?

The thought raced through her head just before what felt like a baseball bat cracked into her leg. It had hit her just above her shoe but before the break in her leg. Another yelp of pain escaped her lips, this time, deliberately.

A few choice curses helped alleviate the sudden surge of pain.

Whether it was from the sun, dehydration, the fall, her broken leg or her snake bite, the world spun away...

"No, absolutely not," the curator had said, the answer given even before Jess asked. He had to squeeze through stacks of crates in a bid to greet her at his door.

Maxwell wasn't a malicious man, he just knew where the money came from. Tall, with wavy black hair and an expensive black suit, he had headed her off as soon as she'd appeared at his doorway, peering into a busy office with rows of metal shelves teaming with boxed artifacts and overflowing with paperwork. She managed to make it in a few feet by the time he'd snaked through the make-shift path.

"Liaoning is where I need to go," Jess was adamant. "It's where the most exciting discoveries are being made."

Maxwell shook his head, letting loose a choppy laugh. "Why should this museum fund an expensive expedition when your paleontological exhibits barely pass a profit?"

"China has birds. Dinosaurs more birdlike than ever discovered. Birds, Maxwell. Birds!" No American was ready to take a step back into the Cretaceous. If they did, they wouldn't find dumb, lumbering lizards there, but more likely small, feathered theropods, perhaps brightly colored for mating. Intelligent, active, social creatures.

Vibrant.

It'd be more like the Tiki Room at Disneyland, but with less singing. The flowers were debatable. Pre-Magnolias and broad leaf species of veriforman were the purview of a paleobotanist--

"No, no, dinosaurs had their shot. They're extinct. Not birds. Maybe to you, maybe to me. But to the people who visit… they're lazy turtles and terrible lizards. If you want to bring them back to life, change the way people think these creatures, then get them in front of the camera." Maxwell chuckled again, "Indy- uh… *Indiana Jones and the Lost World.*"

"Dammit Disney," Jess cursed under her breath. Disney was more than just theme-park attractions. They had successfully captured the imagination of children the world over because they could tell a story like none other. Stories that made them a fortune and dictated the cultural landscape of her generation.

"Put someone in front of a camera long enough," Maxwell said, "Let them spin enough stories, they can shape the planet. It's not just the stories themselves, but who gets to tell them that matters."

He was right, Jess knew. The problem was no one had ever bothered to put a plausibly accurate version of *Tyrannosaurus* in front of an audience in over 66 million years. No recent books, no movies, no one had slapped it on a damned lunchbox either. "I should have been an archeologist."

"You don't mean that." Maxwell was more than just the museum's director to her. He had been on her thesis board too. She had little desire to dig up mummies, and he knew the reason why. One of the few who did. He'd even been the one to suggest the tattoo on her wrist.

Maxwell had been a cultural anthropologist before he became a Suit. Focusing on the earliest stories and their importance. "Beer and cave paintings," he argued. The root of civilization.

"Go somewhere local," Maxwell said dismissively. "Bring back one of your birds. Maybe you can change public opinion one museum guest at a time. But make sure to bring me something *big*."

It was hopeless to convince Maxwell to fund her expedition to China. *Like arguing with Lucas*, as the recent meme went.

People had once clamored for a new *Star Wars* flick. Even Disney had thrown their cash at George. Still, he wouldn't budge, except to cash in a few tech properties and his stake of *Indiana Jones*. "*The technology just doesn't exist to tell future Star Wars stories the way I want to,"* he'd say. *"It's not for sale."*

Without any new stories in a galaxy far, far away for the next generations, it didn't matter that the technology had finally caught up. Except for a few holdouts like herself, no one cared about *Star Wars* anymore. That saga had ended.

"Stories matter," Maxwell would argue. She'd heard it before. "A single story can change the world. But the corollary is that stories are generational. Stop telling it for a while, especially if it's an oral tradition, and it's just dust in the wind."

Jess held in a groan. She wanted to get mad at him for denying her request. But she couldn't. They'd probably go out to a bar tonight, listen to Randy Newman on the jukebox (his choice, not hers) and drink a few beers.

She could press it further then. He'd probably turn a bottom of Jameson upside down and go on his usual rant about Hollywood stars turned politicians.

"It's because we let them make shit up," he'd explain. "Take Schwarzenegger. After *Terminator* and the stupid success of *The Last Action Hero*," he'd probably take a swig for dramatic effect, "and a whole string of muscle-bound *manly* action movies after it, 'The Governator' shouldn't have surprised anyone. But strongarming his goddamned cronies in Congress to pass an amendment?" By then, he'd be slurring, "President goddamned Schwarzenegger."

It could be worse.

This was typical of their arguments. She'd start with the taxonomy of *Tyrannosaur* species and they'd end up talking about why Marvel never made any movies.

"We can discuss where I'm digging later," Jess said, backing out of the office, deftly avoiding a stack of papers perched halfway on an elbow-high shelf.

Maxwell wasn't so lucky, smashing one of his Italian leather shoes into a crate, scuffing it. He let loose a flavorful string of sounds that weren't quite curses. "My answer isn't going to change. Dig somewhere affordable. Find something huge or I'm using your wing for storage. That's final. You don't want to end up a bitter old drunk like Horner."

Jess recalled the former paleontologist. He'd had a few famous finds and been on a few documentaries. With more funding or public support, he could have been the face of paleontology. Or that eccentric Bakker guy, the one with the big book. Neither had acclimated themselves well to obscurity and failure. And she sure as hell didn't want to end up like them. *Hell Creek it is, then.*

She slunk her head in surrender, wondering what her brother would think of all this, the one who'd helped save her and set her on this path.

The prairie rattler grew bored. The sun had dipped from its noontime high, and the wind whipped through the ravine. As the snake slithered away, it gave Jess one last disapproving glare, then went off in search of a meal or burrow for the night.

"What, where you goin' little guy?" Jess propped herself back up on her elbows and watched as the snake left her company. "I was just starting to like you."

She doubted the snake had envenomated her much, it was a precious commodity to them, after all. And she was clearly not a meal.

It could have been worse. If she had stumbled off a cliff and fallen through a mysterious gateway to the Mesozoic. With dinosaurs chirping and rumbling about. A snake was nothing compared to being *Dilophosaurus* dinner.

Alright, humor in check. That's step one. Maintain a positive attitude. It's not too bad, right?

Her leg throbbed and her head spun, but she could manage if she focused. And she had to focus. Otherwise, she wasn't leaving Hell Creek.

Ever.

She dug her phone out of a leg pocket. The screen was cracked. No, the fall hadn't broken her phone, she'd done that a long time ago on the tile floor in the bathroom. Still, she frowned, no signal.

I need a plan. She thought her actions out, as calmly as she could, addressing each problem at a time.

First, she took off her black tank top to reveal a black sports bra underneath. She tied the shirt around her leg just above the snakebite. Slow the venom, if any.

She took her chalk bag belt and cinched it around her leg, letting slip a yelp, thankful it hadn't been a compound fracture. *Or I'd be dead.*

She wasn't sure if she had gotten the order right, and with the chemicals rushing through her system, from adrenaline to toxins, it was possible she'd made a mistake. But it was the best she could do under the circumstances.

Looking around, she saw nothing she could improvise as a splint. Which would mean hell for her leg for the long journey back.

But first, she needed water. Desperately. Her glasses and her canteen hadn't bothered to make the journey with her downhill. She looked around for her rock hammer, cursing that it too had been separated from her by the fall.

She remembered from looking over the edge that there was a dry stream bed below. Now, she was on top of it. She inched over the tough prairie earth and in between two juniper bushes among a long, thin line of shrubs.

Dry.

But, not underneath, she was sure.

She examined the hard earth and then her hands, sighing. Tiny, dull fingertips wouldn't be enough. There were rocks scattered about but none nearby and she needed that water *now.*

I need my hammer. It was dull on one side, pointed like a pickax on the other. A paleontologist's primary tool. But she had something else that might work.

With a spark of an idea in mind, she removed her raptor claw from the chalk bag, and dug the sharp end into the dirt. She imagined a *Dakatorapter* giving her a disapproving look. Still, it worked. Within minutes, she had dug down deep enough for water to pool. She drank at it, greedily.

Thanks, Big Bro. Sam had given her the claw as a gift when she had decided to pursue paleontology, shortly after her incident. This was the second time he had saved her life.

Her thirst slaked, it was as good a time as any to stand. She used her good knee and hands to hoist herself upright. To her own surprise, it didn't hurt nearly as much—

She cried out as her leg resettled into its new position.

Never mind. Oh, this is gonna be fun.

Still, she stood. And she could ambulate, as evidenced by a slow, steady hobble toward the crags.

On any given day, she could scramble up it, minimal effort required. But looking at it, in the narrowing window of daylight, the once-ragged cliff face looked to her as smooth as obsidian.

"Get closer, the imperfections, tiny, imperceptible cracks in the surface will appear," her brother had taught her. Still, it looked impossible.

What she needed was a chimney climb. Something she could put her back against to allow her leg a chance to rest. After some searching, as the air quickly cooled and purple-orange fire burst across the sky, she found a way.

I hope.

It was two cliff faces side by side, a few feet apart and about twenty feet up to the top. Easy enough on a difficult day.

Today was a terrible one. Perhaps tragic.

Here goes nothing.

She placed her back against one cliff's edge, wedging her good foot against the other. With a grunt, a red-face, and some effort, she brought her bad leg up and found purchase for her ankle. It was just a matter of putting her weight on it and moving her good leg up.

Rinse and repeat.

She took short quick breaths to muster up the courage.

With a scream, she managed it.

After time and effort, her skin was slick with sweat, her head dizzy. Her lips were puffy and swollen, probably from the bit of venom her friend had left her.

Still, looking down as the sun disappeared, she'd managed about ten feet. Half the climb.

It wasn't until she looked skyward, at the distance still to go, that she began to cry.

If it had just been the snake bite or the fall, I might have made it. But both? Who could have predicted that?

Was all this effort to survive worth it? As the last light faded, she took a hard look at the semi-colon tattoo on her wrist.

Am I going to die?

It wasn't the first time that question had fleeted through her thoughts.

She awoke in a bed, but it wasn't her bed. She was younger by a few years, perhaps. Tubes and wires stretched everywhere. Bandages wrapped tightly around her wrist. A beeping echoed across the sterile, bright hospital room.

She was in a memory. A bad place.

A door opened, in walked her brother. With a slow nod her way, he started, "I'm here for you with an ear. Two of 'em if you'd like." Sam sat down by her side on the hospital bed. There was a package on his lap.

"I'm so sorry, Sam," Jess had tried to explain. It wasn't her fault that she sometimes felt a certain way. But how to express that? She hadn't meant to—

Just because you can do something, doesn't mean you should, her therapist had told her.

"You don't ever have to explain anything. I understand." He offered her the package. She opened it, letting the wrapping fall to the floor.

It was a wooden puzzle. The three-dimensional kind. She looked at it cockeyed. "What is it?"

"It's a *T-Rex*." The picture on the box showed the wooden model upright, two tiny little arms flailing, its tail on the ground for support. "It's what the package says anyway. I remember you liking dinosaurs as a kid."

She opened the box eagerly, though it was painful to move her wrist. Her lips upturned into a slight smile.

"There's more to your story," Sam said. "We're gonna do puzzles anytime you need an ear. Whatever it takes to get you through each chapter."

She wondered why she hadn't thought about dinosaurs since. Maybe she should start thinking of them again...

When she was a little, *Archaeopteryx* was her favorite. She liked the artist's rendering of bright colored feathers, though her teachers had said that it wasn't a dinosaur and had discouraged further talk. Archeology was the domain of muscle-bound men in fedoras, after all.

Jess looked at her brother wordlessly and began to weep.

Venus was out by the time Jess had finished resting, perched within the crags of the cleft.

I'm not going to give up. There is more to my story.

She reached out a hand, the one that had once been bandaged, the one with the tattoo of the semi-colon. She found a place on the opposing rock face to find a grip.

But something about it didn't feel right.

She brushed her hand over the spot, several times, feeling it out. It was smoother than the surrounding surface...

Jess carefully extricated her phone out of her pants pocket and flipped on the flashlight feature.

Out of the rock, a narrow snout and a toothy grin flashed out at her.

Her heart exploded, adrenaline bursting through her body. She nearly slipped and fell, which would have been the death of her.

After a deep breath. she shone the light on the discovery, and this time, her heart leapt again, but for joy.

Skull intact, looks good. A specimen of raptor?

A *Dakotaraptor?*

Excitement coursed through her veins. *Or was that the venom?*

A stray thought hit her. *What if that had been real? Alive?* Could they bring dinosaurs back to life? Should they? She mulled it over, using those thoughts to help work through the pain, and wondering if she really did ever want to come face-to-face with a raptor at night.

Okay, I'm not giving up. I owe it to my brother. Myself. And this girl here.

"Bring back something," Max's voice rang in her head. *Something to save my wing of the museum.*

This was certainly a find, she thought, as she edged herself up the cliff, grimacing with each movement of her leg. Was this her answer?

No.

Sure, the skeleton was worthy of excavation and study, but that wouldn't turn the tide for her. She had been wrong. The skeleton wasn't what she had been searching for all this time.

The inklings of an idea flooded her mind. A real solution. *A single story can change the world.*

As she dove into the myriad thoughts circling in her head, the climb became easier, as a lost world emerged.

Finally, she grasped dirt at the top of the cliff and pulled herself up. Still, she kept going, forcing herself to stand. It had been an hour from her Jeep to the cliff.

She knew it wouldn't be an hour back. As she ambled on, busy thoughts kept her pain at bay.

All that was left of the dinosaur's legacy was bone. And a bone was just a puzzle piece to a larger story, so long as someone told it. *I will. I think I have an idea to capture the imagination the world over…*

Jess shoved open the door to her jeep and collapsed inside.

After gulping down the contents of her spare canteen, and popping several aspirin from her med kit, she started the ignition. When it roared to life, she kissed the steering wheel.

I've survived.

Again.

"I'm going to write the damned story," she said to no one in particular. Her near escape from death had given her a kernel of a character in mind. Her journey gave her a plot. And her ascent had helped form her thoughts. *A woman on an island. Full of biological attractions. Until something goes wrong, and she must survive the dangers.* "Get a *Rex* and a few bird-like raptors in front of a camera. Bring the dinosaurs back to life." *A story to change people's perceptions.*

Jessica Yang, PhD, knew what to do after once again considering the tattoo on her wrist; the daily reminder that she had attempted to punctuate her life short, but she was still here, living each day as another page. From the moment with her brother and that *Rex* puzzle, to her raptor claw and her museum exhibits, she'd found something to help combat her daily struggles.

Dinosaurs had helped me continue my story. I'll help them continue theirs.

The sun edged over the horizon of Hell Creek, washing over the formation with its first rays of morning light. The Jeep lurched forward, kicking up a chaotic cloud of dust.

As Jess drove off into the sunrise, the dust of the earth settled in a wholly new, unpredictable path.

End.

Notes for Dust of the Earth

You may have noticed a trend here. Yet another story from a childhood inspiration. Authors are sponges. What inspires us, what fills our blank slate, is whatever water we've soaked in from our surroundings (and similarly, writing is much like wringing). I've always loved dinosaurs as a child. Most of us did. But I never grew out of that phase. I read Bakker and Horner and went to any bone museum I could. And then came Michael Crichton's *Jurassic Park*.

His book would spawn 6 global blockbusters across two generations, a TV series, videogames, theme-park attractions, and countless lunchboxes worldwide. Perhaps more important than its pop-culture importance is how it has vividly brought to life dinosaurs to our collective imagination. The terrifying *Tyrannosaur*, the gentle giants like *Brachiosaur*, and the cunning intelligence of raptors. Crichton, on the backs of all those hardworking paleontologists, brought back bones out of the dust of the Earth and shaped them for us with his story, thus giving a bygone era a new lease on life.

But what if Michael Crichton never wrote *Jurassic Park*?

This story was originally published in *Tales From Alternate Earths 3* from the award winning Inklings Press.

Mandela

Two hours.

A slogging two hours since my last fix.

I was alone in the house that day, a custom-built desert dwelling; a ranch-style home that had once been occupied by a pillar of our small community. I was anything but. The wife was gone for work. And I was busy with mine.

Assuming, of course, that work meant avoiding writing while sitting in your PJs, on a comfy chair, your mind on porn, or ensnared in the latest Netflix binger. Both equate to about the same thing anyway, if you think about it. Try not to. Thinking leads to choice and choices weren't an option anymore.

Yet, sitting there in my malaise didn't bring me any closer to my fix.

I put the TV on pause and pulled out my tablet, trembling fingers stumbling around the power button, nearly dropping the thinking machine on the hard-tiled floor. I breathed in as the device powered on, shut my eyes to the soft start-up tones and a soft, artificial voice greeted me with, "Welcome, Brent."

As the screen refreshed and connected to the web, I breathed out heavily to the latest trending tags and click-bait headlines and opinion pieces on news sites devoid of objectivity (who needs that anyway?) and pictures of foods I'd never eaten from places I'd never visit from friends I didn't really know.

Soon, I'd settle into the dopamine dose of comments seen, posts liked, blue birds twittering away – my virtual voice heard.

Relaxed, in the moment of Zen, a local weather widget warned of an approaching storm. It rained now. A lot. Sometimes snowed. The weather had turned severe last winter and looked like it would this

December too. Desert sands were mud. Joshua Trees were gone. No one had seen a tortoise in the wild in years.

I could have checked the source. Gone to a different website to verify. Looked out the damned window. Spoon-fed, I did no such thing, but switched the tablet off to do what everyone does at news of big winter weather landing hard on soft bodies. I put on pants and headed to the store, confident that my own self-absorption would shelter me from any interaction, like a mask or a flu-like fog might obfuscate you from the world.

I could have walked. The supermarket wasn't that far. Though walking meant running the risk of talking to neighbors or strangers or having a moment of self-introspection that could only lead to trouble.

Arriving at the store, I saw that it was packed by everyone else on their own little highs, their own little micro-doses of the world. It all made sense. They saw the same weather forecast online and reacted the same as I had. Choice was a luxury long lost somewhere to time.

I had just passed the bananas in the produce aisle, just beyond the bakery, when the holes in space and time opened. Snowflake-like fractals cracked and spread across empty air at the shelf level of Little Debbie snack cakes. The pattern stretched, the way you might pry apart stage curtains and peer out to see the audience on the other side.

In reality, it was more like a sheet of ice thawing on a sunny day. Given the hole's icy appearance, those annoying trending tags simply dubbed them, "The Frost," after the poet who wrote about paths in a wood diverging. The gateways were mirrors, in a way, a reflection of yourself in an alternate world.

Ever since scientists and sci-fi writers were proved right about The Big Rip, holes were just a thing that happened. Most of us didn't understand the how. Just that our universe neared its death after its explosive expansion and, as a result, was stretching and ripping itself apart at its end.

Yet the scientists were startled to discover something else: It wasn't just us. There were other universes too.

Imagine a stack of pancakes. Each one a mirror of our own universe, atop each other, infinitely. The entire multiverse had expanded, each one at minutely different rates. As each one stretched and ripped, you could see holes form, from one parallel world to the next, as if they were slices of Swiss cheese all slightly askew.

Seeing a wormhole, or a tear in the fabric of space and time, was about as common now as witnessing a shooting star on a crystal-clear night. Assuming, of course, you were cosmically attuned to see such a sight. I guess some people just saw things differently than others.

For instance, I was a Look-See. When the wormholes came, I could look, see the people I might have become had I taken their paths, made their choices instead of my own. Sounds cool, right?

Trust me, it wasn't any sort of gift. There's no joy in knowing that in every version of you that exists in the universe, you led much the same life. That Swiss cheese metaphor I was talking about earlier doesn't vary much from one slice to the next. You're almost never a rock star. It doesn't work like that. Probably for the best.

I passed the busy Little Debbie aisle, Moon Pies in hand, oddly unafraid at the cracking, icy wormholes opening down each aisle of Stater Brothers.

Afterall, I had Diet Pepsi to stock up on. And Red Baron frozen pizza. And of course, a bottle of Crown Royale Apple Whiskey. Maybe toilet paper. For those were the supplies I sought when the storms came. I felt smug in my superiority that I wasn't grabbing the same groceries as everyone else, completely oblivious that in the scheme of things, Red Barons or Tostinos, Coke or Pepsi, there wasn't really a choice at all.

Looking down from my cart at what should have been the baking aisle, I saw myself. He was a healthier version of me. Slimmer, in activewear, with a blue hand basket instead of a cart, and there were big green leafy things flowering over the edge, things that I could not recognize. He turned away from me, unaware of either myself or the fact that he was in a tunnel of icy, coalescing fractals, converging from his reality into mine.

I nodded to the Not-Me, happy for my slight pudge around the waist. Fit Me wasn't Fun Me, I was sure. *He must be miserable.*

The next aisle over crackled with a different tear in time and space and a different me. This me looked the same, but with a different woman by his side than the usual tall dirty blonde with the big brains and soft smile that could kick my ass on her worst day and me on my best.

This woman was shorter, blonder, and a little too into caked-on make-up and gaudy jewelry for my taste. I wondered how this Not-Me and her had met, who she was, how'd they'd come together instead of the happiness I had found. He didn't look any better off. I'm sure he was miserable. If I'd found the love of my life, surely, he couldn't have.

A young woman in yoga pants and a loose-fitting Cal-State sweater passed me while I watched myself down the aisle. She turned, passed through the vision of me and that other wife, and disappeared somewhere behind them, completely unawares.

She might have been one of the few who couldn't see the rips in reality. Who had no awareness of their alternate-selves. There were others, like her, who didn't see anything at all. As a result, they all had something in common: they still strived for greatness, emboldened by a world of choice in which they might succeed.

They were the worst off, because they lived in ignorance. So, they thought and acted and made choices and did all the things we used to do before we knew better. I almost pitied her. Such a waste of efforts.

I was better off in seeing my different fates. None of them were particularly impressive. Others who were like me, who experienced holes and breaks in space-time, who saw themselves cast in a different light in an alternate reality readily agreed.

With few exceptions, like the writer who got the breakout book, the singer with the sudden hit song, there were simply too many factors that relegated us all to the same minor set of circumstances, like crabs in a bucket that pulled each other down. Too many societal issues that locked us away in invisible cages.

In a sea of infinity, most of us swam endlessly in mediocrity through no choice or fault of our own.

Occasionally, I saw myself with a smile. Signing autographs at the bookstore instead of buying another Stephen Baxter book. Not in a vegetative state getting my high with my tablet thumbed to the newest social media posts, but busily clacking away at a keyboard in earnest effort to create my own reality, my own fate. In those cases, sure, I wished I might be a Mandela.

They had it the best.

Have you ever thought some tiny detail wasn't quite right, or have you remembered something only slightly different than everyone else? Maybe you live in a reality where you're not aware that the universe was ripping itself apart.

Yet, you're affected all the same; if you thought Nelson Mandela died in prison, thought the Fruit of the Loom label looked off, if you thought chartreuse was pink in color, or if you saw Sinbad as *Shazaam* – you've slipped streams, gone from one reality to another. You might be a Mandela.

I'm jealous. You might just keep slipping streams, like salmon bucking the current, until you arrive precisely in the reality you want most.

For the rest of us, we were stuck. I was unable to move from one reality to another. I lived with strangers wearing my face; reflections of choices I had made only to reach roads not all that dissimilar to my own. It was rather depressing.

Case in point, down the snack aisle, I saw myself once more. Not fit or with a different spouse by my side, not richer or poorer, but as myself, as I was now, with matching items in our carts, the same Nike shoes with one lace that kept coming undone. I wondered just what odds created a mirror so exact in likeness that I could see myself in its reflection, and I trembled at the idea that in an infinite galaxy, there were most likely more of me just like myself in every detail than I ever wanted to admit.

At home again, with the Crown Royale opened on my desk and groceries stocked in preparation for a storm that was only promised to come, I was away from the wormholes, away from my alternate selves, and back in comfort. Safe.

Yet, my nerves jittered, and my tablet called to me.

With all our choices laid bare, all our options seen like reflections in a fun-house mirror, there wasn't anything to ever do but to trudge along. No matter what choices we made, we could see firsthand that it didn't really matter, that no paths taken would ever make our lives that different than our own.

The rips in space-time had come and taken our free will away.

So, most of us lived from one fix to the next. Tolerating reality in the smallest doses, a reality that had been warped and bubbled and twisted to fit our needs and wasn't really real anymore anyway. We were happy and content in that bubble where choices couldn't harm us.

I looked anxiously at my watch. It had been close to two hours since my last fix.

End.

Notes for Mandela

Okay, so this story is really all Rudy Rucker's fault. He's the science fiction author behind the transrealism movement and this was my attempt at dipping my toes in the genre. While I think the story came out okay, the cool thing is Mandela originally aired on Simultaneous Times Podcast episode #23 along with the story "Fat Stream" by none other than Rudy Rucker himself.

Twilight of the Mesozoic Moon

"Gon'… of Tribe Rak," the words echoed like an alarm clock against the cement floor of the barracks. Gon'rak's eyelids cracked open, black-amber pupils dilating in the dark room. Even through the grogginess, he could tell the words were laced with authority, underscored by a low, guttural growl. He didn't have any choice but to respond.

But that didn't mean he had to hurry. His eyes drifted closed again while he rose from his balanced, vertical sleeping stance, placing his clawed foot down and stretched out his arms, ruffling his feathers. He took his time, so that whomever had awakened him would realize who was really in charge here.

He could tell through his eyelids that moonlight was already spilling in through the window. *Time to get up anyway*, he grumbled to himself. But when he lifted his eyelids once more, he was met with eyes staring directly at his, not a full tail-length in front of his snout.

Out of instinct, his oversized toe-claw popped up. He began to coil onto his hind legs. He opened his mouth, displaying a row of razor-sharp teeth—and probably a major case of bad breath. He wasn't as well-built as the other *Theros* standing in front of him, but he wouldn't give in without leaving a few scars he thought, before realizing his would-be attacker hadn't even moved a claw.

It was only then when Gon'rak noticed there were *two* of them, one just a step outside his periphery. But they both had the bearing and feather-colors of Imperator Soldiers—the last fact he could barely discern in the dim room. The odds didn't look good. *What were they doing here?*

"Pilot Gon'rak, you are needed immediately," the first soldier said in the staccato tapping of an oversized toe-claw on the smooth, hard floor. Technically, Gon'rak was an Imperator soldier as well, and his tribal ranking wasn't too low. But having Imperator guards in his small, no-hatchling hovel was a step or six above his standing. He briefly wondered what this was all about, but he knew better than to ask. Hell, if this had to do with the project he'd been kicked out of, "asking" was the last thing he should do. Gon'rak didn't respond at all as he was led outside and into the dawning rays of the Two-Headed moon.

On most nights, he would have ignored the moon, with its extensive crack, just as he always did. The Two-Headed God knew it. But as he found himself sprinting along a familiar path leading from his Spartan barracks to the lavishly-built rocket observatory, he couldn't help stealing glances at it.

The moon was as it always had been. Large, luminous, but for dark shadows caught in between the deep crevices of its crack. The fissure ran down its western ridge, carving the faces where the Two-Headed God dwelt. The Gods had been there for as long as their civilization had known. And the *Theros* worshiped Them for just as long, Gon'rak figured. They all seem to have trusted the Wise and the Jester to keep together. The Imperator had promised as much. But Gon'rak guessed there was something more at work than the word of their leader.

Gon'rak was not an astronomer. But he did know what the astronomers, like his friend Car'ren, told him. The crack was caused by an asteroid which the moon caught 66 million years ago. It never quite fused back together. Worse, the earth's gravitational pull would eventually rip it apart. All it needed was some small shove. And knowing that made Gon'rak dangerous.

The Imperator, for obvious reasons, chose to keep the secret close. Gon'rak could understand the need to contain panic among the masses. And of those who knew? Well, the Imperator's "plan", Gon'rak grumbled to himself, was apparently enough to keep the peace.

Whatever that plan was. He'd been summarily dismissed from it and kept under close scrutiny ever since. Until tonight. And it seemed tonight just might be the end of the world, he realized. The terror of that thought tugged at his mind.

The tugging brought him back to when he was a hatchling, when Gon'rak gazed at the moon for hours. He wanted to be there, when the moon was whole, to see it as one. He wanted to be in the jungle with his ancestors. Instead, he settled for seeing their bones in museums. It was always the big ones, the ones that the ancient *Theros* killed off that he liked the most. The Tyrannosaurs, the Triceratops, and the massive long-necked sauropods. He'd stare at the dry bones for as long as his mother would allow.

And back at his home, he would go straight back to staring at the moon. Especially when he was sad. The night he learned of his mother's murder, Gon'rak didn't take his eyes off the heavens for an instant. But the sky was full of blackness. There were no Gods that night.

His father came to him. Gon'rak rested his head on his father's feathery chest. "Dad," Gon'rak had asked, "Why do the Gods not come every night?"

He was afraid his father would tell him the same story about the moon landing. About how they stepped foot on the Gods. From that, they knew the Gods were with them, even when they could not be seen. Instead, his father was quiet, and in the barest click of his toe, he answered softly, "Gods come when times are darkest."

It hadn't made sense to him, and it didn't make sense now. *The Gods were here tonight, in full view of all Theros. Yet they were going to break apart and rain down death on this planet. Gods be damned.*

The Imperator Rex had no use for bone-diggers, but he did have use for soldiers. Gon'rak trained to be a pilot and passed the tests. His abilities were more than capable, but his questioning of certain things made him a liability.

Apparently, that wasn't enough to stop the Imperator from calling him here tonight. And, as he pondered, he reached the white-cement structure connected to the egg-shaped observatory, just as other participants of their mission came rushing out.

Among them were the Twins, with their identical purple plumage and habit for finishing each other's thoughts. Had Gon'rak known he was going to be the pilot for tonight, he would have taken better care to remember their respective names. His feathers twitched in self-reproach. The Twins continued down the path, while another scientist stood sniffing the air and turned toward him. There was no problem at all remembering her name.

The two guards lowered their snouts at Gon'rak in dismissal, and darted off toward another area of the compound, just as Car'ren approached. "It's happening now," she said hurriedly. "There is a meteor shower raining down on the far side of the moon and the moon is close enough tonight to let Earth's gravity do the rest—" She looked him over, as if taking a second to realize why it was him standing there and not someone else.

She winked, knowingly. "That's right! I heard our head pilot was sick. Terrible timing, that is. Luckily, we have you." She switched from claw-tapping to talking and he knew what she was about to say. "We can watch it from here, for as long as the Overseer allows, or up safely on the ship."

As the Twins darted down the path across the observatory to where Gon'rak knew the launch pad for the Chronus was, he eyed Car'ren carefully. She was a rarity. She had a habit for dreaming big. And a worse habit for wanting to make those dreams become real. There were not many women scientists. *There were not that many scientists.* The Gods did not allow it. But tales of her advancements kept the Imperator Rex looking the other way, despite the enemies she'd made to get here. As a result, he'd heard her tail feathers were tough, as the saying went.

But Gon'rak was not intimidated by her; in fact, he found her fascinating. "I'd rather see it with my own eyes, with you." His tail twitched, feathers ruffled, and both turned their snouts skyward.

It happened almost instantly. At first, the moon shone, bright and beautiful, and a moment after that, the crack began to fissure, and the moon began to slowly crumble. Bit by bit, rocks dislodged and drifted off, caught in a gravity tug-of-war that the Earth would ultimately win—and lose at the same time.

The fissure widened. And—without a sound—the moon continued to crack into larger and larger pieces and peeled away from the core. Strangely—for a moment—the pieces remained suspended, as if it were an unfinished jigsaw puzzle, just as his heart seemed to hang within the hole in his chest. Even the ornithos stopped chittering in the trees. The sky was quiet, but he could hear the gasps and squawks starting from the once-sleeping city below.

Even though Car'ren once told him it would take an hour or two for the first bits of rock to reach the Earth's surface, Gon'rak couldn't help that his head-feathers rose in fear, and he ticked his head back to check that the shuttle was still there.

From behind, there came a series of several high-pitched horn-bursts. It was unmistakably the Overseer, shouting at them to enter the shuttle. But they ignored the command and stood there awhile longer, caught in the moment of the cataclysm. "This is always what you wanted to do, right? Be a pilot?" Car'ren asked him by way of clicks and taps of her over-sized toe-claw.

"Not really, I wanted to be a bone-digger," he replied. "But I can fly. It's just that…"

"What?" She asked.

There were more horn bursts. Any other *Theros* would have already been there, tail and snout down, at the ready. But not her. Not him, for that matter, as he found himself still standing there, staring at her.

"It doesn't feel right, leaving the rest of them like this," he answered, guiltily. "I mean, I'm not even the primary pilot, and how many of us are on the mission? Half-dozen? Aren't you the only woman, I mean, what are we supposed to do up there?"

If Car'ren could have shown embarrassment, she would have, Gon'rak realized with some embarrassment of his own. Instead, her thin golden feathers, which traced a radiant outline down her sides, seemed to spark against the fiery horizon. "There's more to the mission than you know. As the Overseer would say, 'the Imperator Rex is wise'. You'll have to trust me."

Gon'rak couldn't put his faith in the Imperator. Car'ren didn't seem to either. So instead, he ticked his head sidewise, stared at her for a long moment with one eye, then darted down the same path that led from the observatory to the *Chronus*. Car'ren followed behind.

* * *

The launch pad was deliberately made to look like nothing special. In this narrow stretch of land, surrounded by the East Salt Sea, shuttle launches like this one were common. However, this shuttle was different from the ones launched at this site before. The main rocket itself was the same design—long and slender, tapered at the end, like a big white hand of a clock. But surrounding it was something like a sleeve, or a cuff, which wrapped around the rocket. Gon'rak never figured out what the cuff was for, but it made the sleek ship ungainly and bulky to pilot during the simulations. He doubted the real thing would prove any easier.

Gon'rak silently passed by the white and black feathers, dyed in the manner of the moon, as befitted a representative of the Two-Headed God and the Imperator Rex. The Overseer eyed him but remained silent. Instead, he snapped at Car'ren. "The moon is breaking apart, falling from the sky, and you delay? Our mission is sacred," he intoned with head feathers raised threateningly, "when I command, you come."

Car'ren's composure did not change. "Is Captain Gno'res onboard?"

The Overseer ticked his head.

"Good. I'll check in with him."

He hissed in return as she disappeared through the door.

Gon'rak should have kept going, but he found himself bobbing backwards, spurred on by Car'ren's courage. "What, you'll tell the Imperator? He's not around. He had the tail-feathers to stay here and share the same fate as his people."

There was a reason Gon'rak wasn't the first choice for pilot, he knew, as the words fell from him. "We have no need of an Overseer on this ship," he continued with some small measure of confidence. Normally, words like that would mean death. But with the sky falling all around him, there was little else to fear.

"Get in," the Overseer growled, plumage raised, toe-claw cocked. But he remained still.

Gon'rak felt proud of himself, though the feeling was short lived. He looked over his shoulder at the shattered sky, as his heart slowed and sank. It would likely be the last time he would see the Earth as he knew it.

The fog was already dense as he made his way through dim red lighting and across the corrugated steel floors of the ship. The wet atmosphere felt good on his dry feathers. And his dust and dander would be less likely to drift into sensitive electronic equipment.

Tiny, brown-feathered Troodons clung to the pitted floors of the ship, claws finding easy purchase on the floor, giving them an adequate foothold in which to leap high to pluck dragonflies and wasps from the heavy air. As Gon'rak found his way to his seat, his belly moaned, reminding him he hadn't eaten yet, as the snacks scurried too closely near his claws. He eyed a nearby Troodon hungrily.

Before he could snatch it up, a voice interrupted him. "Pilot Gon'rak, prepare yourself, time is fleeting." This command came politely from the captain in the usual toe-clicks used to convey respect instead of what that the Overseer used. *See? Not that hard.* Gon'rak had always liked the captain. He ignored his empty stomach and moved along.

The rocket was nearly prepped, he found, as he collapsed backward against a back brace that would provide support during take-off. A seat hissed up beneath him, surrounding his tail. Gon'rak swung the control panel parallel to his odd angle and he would be ready to pilot the ship once all the systems checked out. Assuming they were still going to follow all the time-consuming procedures. *Were they going to do that?*

"Gon'rak," Captain Gno'res clicked on a screen with a long series of questions, prompting a response for each of them. "Prepare the pre-flight checklist."

"Captain?" Normally, Gon'rak would settle into the routine. He didn't need the questions. But today he did. "Do we even have time for this?"

"No," the Overseer tapped in what sounded like annoyance. "Launch."

"If we launch now and something goes wrong, the Imperator's plan doesn't work and everybody loses. We have time, if just enough." Gon'rak was envious of the captain's calmness. "Proceed."

What was the Imperator's plan?

He muddled through the checklist as the events thus far kept him wracked with worry. What should have taken half an hour took nearly twice as long. But neither Car'ren nor the Twins gave him any grief. The captain aided Gon'rak through the Overseer's complaints, but eventually, the ship checked out. The Twins noted a couple of colder readings on secondary systems, though there wasn't much they could do about that given the circumstances, they all agreed.

"It's time to go," the captain commanded. "Get us out of here."

The moment he moved the throttle, the shuttle began its controlled explosion skyward. They were off the ground even before the Overseer's seat slid up in place, which earned Gon'rak a squeal of protest. The ship rumbled and vibrated. Gon'rak's teeth and claws clattered. He thought his brain was going to liquefy and pour out of his ears. Only experience taught him that it would all be fine. Soon, the massive rocket would be overcome by the forces lifting it off the ground, the rumbling would stop, and his stomach would return to its original position.

And in fact, a few minutes later, the ship did quiet down. Afterwards, the view screen clicked on. From one of the ship's exterior cameras came a shaky shot of earth. Another monitor showed the rain of fiery rock showering down from the sky. Earth, in its final hour, looked so serene, so unaware, so finally at peace after tens of thousands of years of violence and division.

The first meteor hit. Gon'rak could hear the sickening sound of the solid rock smacking into the planet despite the distance. The shockwave was lost, however, between the ship's violent vibrations and the shield dampeners designed just for this. But he imagined it all the same.

Soon after, it grew deathly still in the cockpit, as more meteors pelted the earth. They could only watch helplessly as each one hit the ground, sending up an explosion of molten rock and earth. And just like that, his home, his friends, even the first female that he'd nested— all began to vanish in a violent rending of the world.

Silently, *Chronus* broke through earth's atmosphere and into the darkness of the void beyond. Gon'rak could feel himself lose focus. He froze in place, as if a slow paralysis had taken hold.

He couldn't make what just happened seem real, though he'd seen it with his own wide eyes. Even still, it didn't seem possible. Maybe, he thought, looking back at the old bones of the Earth in the museums, he knew death wasn't the end. Life could be carried over through memory, if not spiritually.

But this extinction was different. Who would remember them? There was nothing left to be remembered by. As far as he knew, the people who surrounded him in this ship were the only ones alive in the whole universe. He somehow found the will not to vomit.

As his stomach settled, Gon'rak caught movement from behind. The Overseer said, "It is time." Gon'rak heard the click of restraints being undone as the captain and the Overseer released themselves. He did the same, while the Twins watched—their tails twitching in curiosity—as Gon'rak dug his toe-claws into the pitted floor to escape the zero-gravity effect of space.

While Gon'rak steadied himself, the Overseer and Captain Gno'res both took keys hidden within the painted plumage around their necks. The pair stepped to opposite sides of the control panel. As the keys turned simultaneously, the computer clicked over to a different screen.

Car'ren stepped toward the control panel and began typing with her clawed toes and fingers what seemed to be memorized commands. Her practiced movements made him recall a bit of his own training. At the time, it didn't mean anything: *At all costs, keep the ship off the Earth—don't even hit the atmosphere.* As the words swirled around his thoughts, they made even less sense now. *There is no more Earth. We are alone. We are the last of our kind.*

But what she said next made him forget all that. "The *Chronus* cuff is starting its spin. Co-ordinates for the Mesozoic are confirmed."

There was a deep whirring, and Gon'rak could feel a new piece of machinery switch on. A harsh hum tore swiftly through the hull and ripped through his stomach. "Did I hear that right?"

"Yes," Car'ren replied, seemingly oblivious to his unease. "We are traveling back in time."

* * *

Gon'rak gave a long pause to his thought. "We… we can travel in time?"

Everything he'd ever heard of the feat said that it was impossible. Yet Car'ren was hitting control buttons as if that was precisely what they were doing.

Finally, she responded. "Well, we have some ethical implications to time travel we're still working out, and some serious consequences should the ethics not be heeded; that process I can explore with you later. But as to the theory behind it, in a few minutes, well—it will be a matter of fact. That's my job. You just keep us in one piece as the rest of the ship is likely to tear itself apart."

Concern crept across his jaws. He couldn't tell if she was kidding. But as soon as he sat back down he could feel the controls in his claws tightening. The monitors clicked off, and the red lights dimmed. As the cuff spun faster, his ability to keep the ship still was tested against slippery claws and the sheer panic of being caught so completely off-guard.

"I didn't sign up for this," he slipped out. Technically, he wasn't even supposed to be here at all. A few moments ago, he would have gone up in a cloud of ash, now... *well perhaps now, I haven't been born yet.*

The throttle continued to resist his attempts at controlling it. The sleeve around the ship was moving faster than he ever thought possible, and the hull of the rest of the ship creaked and moaned. If he let go, or if the controls stopped responding to his commands, he was sure the ship would shatter like an egg or careen out of control. He didn't want to find out.

Crrrinnch. Gon'rak jerked toward the sound. It was as if metal ripped away from the ship, and a voice—*one of the Twins?*—sounded out in alarm, "Captain, coolant tank three has been damaged. I repeat, the coolant tank has—"

"Hold it a little longer, how close are we?" The Overseer stepped in. It wasn't so much a question, Gon'rak could tell, but an order to return the appropriate response.

"Just... about...," the Twins were sitting side by side. Gon'rak thought it might have been the one on the right who responded. And anyways, he was busy keeping his heart beating and the craft from spiraling off into space.

Through the stiffness of the controls, he could feel the ship being ripped apart. His arms were getting weaker. But all he could think of was, *were they really traveling through time?* The jerking slowed, the shaking stopped, and the lights grew brighter. "There," the same Twin confirmed.

A collective sigh sounded through the cockpit. Afterwards, as if it had been timed, there was a muffled rupture from somewhere outside the spacecraft.

"Well," the other Twin said, "there goes that coolant tank. The O-rings had been reading cold before takeoff."

Really, was that all it was? There was a bit of incredulous disbelief locked onto his face. He could feel it, and he could see that same face as he turned to examine the rest of the crew—all but Car'ren, of course. She continued to look calm.

Gon'rak would have removed himself from the controls, but he found he'd buried several of his claws deep into the instrument panel. It took a good yank to pry them loose, and as he did, his claws made a high-pitched whine as they scraped up against the metal. Finally free, his arms fell, limp and weary to his sides. He took his inspiration from the crazy scientist and tried to breath normally again.

The troodons which became still during the commotion, resumed foraging, as if nothing had happened. One of them leapt, intending to snatch a wasp out of the air, its flightless feathered arms took off in the zero G. It cocked its head at the unexpectedness of its trajectory, as it shot past its prey.

Finally, there was another loud hum. The Troodon looked annoyed with having missed its meal and when it landed back on the floor it skittered away indignantly as gravitational systems kicked on. In a way, Gon'rak felt like that little animal. He too had launched himself up in the air, and it was only by luck it seemed, that he was back on his clawed feet.

The monitors clicked back on, and Gon'rak found himself somewhere he'd never intended to be. Earth, bright and blue, shone in front of him. He refused to trust his eyes. "Is that what I think it is?"

"Home," Car'ren returned. "But it's not *what*, Gon'rak, it's *when*. It is home, or at least home as it was 66 million years ago, assuming the calculations are correct. Even so, clearly, we've proven that time travel is possible." Her jaws opened in the equivalent of a smile. "We're in the past at a time where our species hadn't yet gained sapience, where—"

"Giants roamed." His heart was that of an eight-year-old. He wanted to see Tyrannosaurs and the giant raptors and…and… He felt foolish and happy all at the same time. Maybe he could even see the moon, whole.

"It's too bad we can't go down there," Car'ren said.

"Why not?" Gon'rak asked, her words dashing his dreams. He realized he'd spoken in protest louder than he'd intended. A look around the room showed that he'd caught the attention of even the

Overseer. Gon'rak would've have slunk down in his seat from embarrassment, but he didn't care what the Overseer thought of him. No… only Car'ren.

"As I mentioned before, there are things we can and can't do in the past."

"Really, like what?" Gon'rak puzzled. How could anything they did leave any mark? Compared to the destruction he'd just witnessed, what they could do to themselves seemed pretty damned insignificant.

Car'ren began clicking her toe-claw loudly, as if irritated. After all, much of this was her project, even if she couldn't claim credit for it as a female. Even so, they all knew it was her. Out of respect, he silenced his foolish questions and listened instead as she said, "It is often the smallest act which has the largest impact," she cocked her head his way before she tapped out, "You weren't even supposed to be here. But a flu virus kept our pilot home. Now, he is dead and you are here—alive for the time being, supposing you keep any further questions to yourself."

Gon'rak could tell that she wasn't quite serious. At least he hoped so. Even so, he never felt as smart as he knew he was. And that only happened when he was around her. Quickly, he said something he'd heard before, something that might show his intelligence, "Like the flap of a wasp's wings."

"Precisely." Her plumage shimmered for a moment adding to the hope that he might have impressed her. "We can't control nature. We can only manage it and hope for the best. Because everything we do to interfere, no matter how small, in some way effects change that is beyond our ability to predict."

She turned her snout slightly to the Overseer, as if voicing her disapproval about something to him. "Anything about us, anything about our mission, anything we carry—either from our germs to our psychological baggage—could effect a tremendously different outcome in this new time—"

"Yes." The Overseer stepped forward. "But you see, we can throw out some of these, 'ethical dilemmas' of yours. They are nonsense. The

Imperator Rex does not deal with such concerns. He is descended from those that have set foot on the Two-Headed God. He sees more clearly than you."

"You can't put your faith in dead gods."

"Though we cannot see the moon at present, our Gods are restored. You will see. Ours is a holy mission, one given to us directly from Them. When our world exploded, They set a path for us to follow, set forth by our Imperator, to save the lives of everyone on Earth. Certainly, as a female is attached to her hatchlings, you could appreciate that—if you hadn't given that up, of course."

"If I hadn't given that up," Car'ren growled, "the Imperator, you and everyone on this ship I designed, wouldn't be here."

"Quite, right." The Overseer said, unperturbed. "That is my point entirely. Survival necessitates innovation and, in your case, the violation of some of our society's most sacred laws. It proves how wise the Imperator was to allow you to continue your studies. It was through his mercy and the instructions of the Gods that we are alive."

"So… we will just drift up here until the end of time? What of us?" Gon'rak wanted to keep quiet, but he felt compelled to change the subject, partly to stop the two from escalating. And part of it was curiosity. They were here. They'd succeeded. *Now what?*

"I assure you, everything is happening as planned," The Overseer said defensively. As if to alleviate any concerns, he backed down although there was clear irritation in his words, a growing anger. "We will not interfere with the moon or Earth. When we are finished with our mission, we will return to our present time and we will discover everything is exactly as we left it," tails twitched around excitedly, as the Overseer continued, "except that our moon will be made whole."

Except that the moon will not have two faces, Gon'rak realized. That meant… he didn't know precisely what that meant, but before he could think on it further, the monitors inside grew dim, as if a dark shadow blanketed the cameras.

"Asteroid?" the sullen captain called to Car'ren. Until now, he'd been abnormally quiet, sulking in the shadow of the domineering Overseer.

Instead of Car'ren answering, one of the two purple-plumed Twins spoke instead. "There she is," he said. "Car'ren got us here, now it's our turn to have some fun. The Twins faced each other gleefully. They pressed a few buttons and all the monitors blinked for a moment, then they showed a zoomed-out shot of the asteroid.

Gon'rak gulped foggy air in response to the sight. Even in this smaller view, the asteroid was the biggest object he'd ever seen within the scope of the moon and the earth. It was pocked, much like the surface of the ship's floor, but each pockmark was the size of a cavern, most of which could have easily swallowed the *Chronus*. The big, reddish-brown rock seemed to defy physics. It flew fluidly across the monitor, a slow beacon of death, as it made its way towards its collision with the moon.

For a second, he swore he saw the moon whole. But the shadow of the giant rock of doom covered the moon in partial darkness. He assumed they were here to stop the asteroid… somehow. But he could not fathom how they would do it. It seemed too large a task, too inevitable to stop. Nervously, he asked Car'ren "Uh, do you have a way… to… I mean, look at that thing."

"That?" Car'ren replied. "Oh, it'll be fun, but it's not really my area of expertise. I'm sure the Twins will correct me if I get anything wrong," they bobbed their heads in agreement at the prompt, "but we are going to need your help."

"Me?" It was his turn to bob his head, but his reaction was mostly born out of confusion.

"You didn't think your part was done?" She let out a cruel laugh, laced with a bitter sweetness. "We will need an expert pilot."

"Yes," the Twins clicked in unison. "The laser can't swivel or angle itself. We didn't have time to give it its own maneuverability. It's bolted to the ship."

"Laser?" Well, Gon'rak thought, at least giant, asteroid-killing lasers are more likely than time-travel. Except that he *hadn't* thought it. He'd said it out loud. *Oops.*

"Who said anything about," One Twin started. The other one finished, "blowing it up? That would only make it worse." The first Twin clarified. "We ran theoretical models using a laser with mass—"

"A laser with mass? You mean a particle beam," The other Twin interjected. "How'd you get through school?"

"I cheated off that girl with the red feathers who sat between us, same as you," the first one said, ignoring him and moving on. "Hell, we even tried a paintball gun to push it off its path. But the asteroid is too big and moving too fast. The laser worked best, although it expends quite a bit more energy."

"So, how does it work?" Gon'rak found himself asking. *I should really learn to keep my snout shut.*

Thankfully, lights on a control panel near the west wall of the cockpit started blinking rapidly. One of the Twins leapt to respond to it. He stood there, turning knobs and taking in readouts. Gon'rak couldn't make tails of it. Finally, the Twin said, "Captain, remember the coolant tank that went 'boom' during the cuff rotation?"

"Repair status?" the captain returned.

"That's just it, the coolant tank is irreparable in the time we have left."

Gon'rak looked back to see confusion creeping up over the captain's snout as he mulled the news over. "How much time to impact?"

"Well, that's the other thing. We calculated an arrival time well before the impact, to ensure room for repairs or adjustments. But all readings indicate that we have only… minutes."

"What?" It was a loud, irritated voice, so Gon'rak knew it was Overseer, who then exploded into a series of heated honks. "Could Car'ren have miscalculated?"

"Not likely, but anything is possible," a Twin answered, nodding briefly to Car'ren. The Twins were now both up and busily moving around, so even if Gon'rak knew their names, he couldn't tell who was who anymore. The Twin continued, "But we didn't know precisely when the impact happened. It was the equivalent of an educated guess. Get here too early, we move forward in time, get here too late, we go back some more."

"We can't go back." The Overseer said. There was a hesitation to his clicking. "Not now. So, deploy the laser." But everyone stopped what they were doing instead, confused at what he'd just said, until he stamped out, "Get it done!"

"Yes sir, I just don't understand, we should have plenty of time," the Twins said together.

"Maybe it's our fault?" Gon'rak said hesitantly. He didn't know why he said it, but things were becoming clearer to him. "Maybe our arrival, the act of coming here, could have, I don't know, pushed, or warped things around us? Maybe we accidentally 'shoved' the rock closer to the moon, or off its path?" He smiled at Car'ren, pleased with himself.

Car'ren shared in the toothy grin. His feathers bristled in response. He would have been happier but for the nagging voice pulling at him. *Why couldn't they time travel?* He shook it off for the moment. There were other things to worry about now.

"The computer shows the asteroid still on target to hit the moon, but the coordinates do seem off a bit. Engaging laser."

"Okay, you're up Gon'rak," Car'ren confirmed. "You pilot the ship where the Twins need you. Keep it steady."

"Indeed." Between the bad feeling left by the Overseer, and the importance of what he was being asked to do, his elation melted away, but he couldn't quite get to a point where he fit in with the rest of the crew's dour mood. It was another reminder of why he didn't belong here.

With that, machines clicked and whirred. He could tell that something in the ship opened up. He pictured a giant laser cannon sliding out of the ship to blast the asteroid out of the sky. He prepped himself mentally as he ground his claws into his control panel, readying for anything.

The monitor showed a small, barely discernible object. There was a series of lights on the side, which began to glow faintly.

"Asteroid engaged."

"Wait, that's it?" Gon'rak blurted out. "That's the laser? It's…it's… *tiny*. Is it even working?"

"Praise the Gods, it is." A Twin answered. "Now, adjust to course 149.8 and slow your speed. This is going to take some time…"

"So, we aren't going to blow anything up?"

Car'ren turned sharply. "We'll blow ourselves up if the laser overheats. With one of the coolant tanks out of commission, we just might."

Gon'rak felt ashamed. He'd asked another stupid question. He'd wondered if his ill counterpart back home had been more informed than him, or if he just didn't know when to keep quiet. Sheepishly, he answered, "I suppose the laser is knocking the asteroid off course, but I didn't think lasers operated that way."

"Forgive me, I see what you are saying," Car'ren said in a soothing voice. It made him feel better once she said those words. "You're right. And we are trying to knock the asteroid off course, to keep it from crashing into the moon or anywhere else. If our calculations are right and you keep the laser steady enough, the asteroid should sail harmlessly into the sun. For that to work, the laser only needs to cut the tiniest hole through the rock. At the speed the asteroid is moving, that insignificant cut will act much like a spoiler, or propeller, slowly changing how the whole rock behaves. One cut, and in 66 million years, our planet lives on."

"The smallest acts…"

"Exactly," Car'ren clicked.

Gon'rak was surprised to find some resistance in his controls. The little laser must have been doing something, because he could tell there was a connection between the craft and the space rock. Even worse, he realized that his movements were affecting the laser. But of course, his feathers picked that moment to begin itching. He shuffled around in his seat, while his tail stuck out, stiff as a board. He couldn't break concentration, no matter how ridiculous he was sure he looked. He only hoped Car'ren wasn't watching.

An alarm blared, and his attention darted to the sound. This warning was loud, unlike the others from earlier. Considering he was in a thin metal tube with nothing but the possibilities of death surrounding him, every unexpected beep or buzzing sent his feathers twitching. This alarm though, raised every quill on his neck. *What was it?*

"The laser is overheating." One of the Twins said, in a calm manner which defied the urgency of the alarm. "No worries, I'll decrease the temperature from coolant number—" The silence confirmed Gon'rak's fears. "Yeah, there is no coolant tank there anymore, is there?" He said, head lowering in a frown.

The other Twin finished the thought, "We have no choice but to shut off the laser, before it overheats."

"Very well," the first Twin agreed, and began to shut it down. The display lights on the monitor started to dim and Gon'rak could feel a tangible release in pressure from the controls. "We will have to make repairs and return to an earlier time to try again."

Car'ren nodded, as did the captain.

But it was the Overseer that stepped into the middle of the cabin, teeth bared, toe talon poised high. "Turn the laser back to full power, complete the mission."

"No!" The captain answered in defiance. "We can complete the repairs and go back and try again—"

"As I said earlier, we cannot," The Overseer said, feathers puffing. "Tom'ras," he called to one of the Twins, "You will bring the laser back to full power."

Tom'ras did has commanded, but as soon as the Twin did so, a loud hum began to fill the steel craft. It sent the tiny Troodons into a panic, scattering them through the fog. Gon'rak felt the tension build back up in the controls, only stronger this time.

"No, there is no reason to risk the safety of my crew," the captain said. His voice was a soft whisper at first, slowly growing into a growl of outright disobedience. Or was it? This was Captain Gon'res' ship, after all. "I saw nothing in the mission parameters that would keep us stuck here, the time cuff is operational, is it not? Unless my reports were misleading…"

"Your reports were incorrect, I'm afraid. We only had enough power for one trip. There was never any plan to head back. How could we? Even if we succeeded, the rest of the planet would never know it. We would be outcasts. We would be giving them time travel, and that gift is not ours to give. That secret belongs only to the Two-Headed God."

"And me," Car'ren said, her cool composure broken, claws extended, "You knew there'd be changes to our timeline, just as I said. You lied."

"Twins, stand down," the captain said, flashing his teeth at the Overseer. "I won't risk this crew until the Overseer explains himself."

A sharp claw tore upwards. The captain's stomach split open. The Overseer's snout darted toward the captain's neck. Gon'rak heard the crack of small bones. Gno'res' body went limp. "I do not explain myself. I speak for the Imperator, which means I speak for the Two-Headed God." His snout dripped with sinew. Several Troodons rushed to the scene, each one darting its head down and coming back up with meaty mouthfuls of the former captain.

Gon'rak wanted to scream out against the horror. But the Overseer turned his attention to Car'ren, as if intending to kill her too. He couldn't allow that. Gon'rak shifted the controls to knock the beast off his feet, which proved harder to do in the simulated gravity and pitted surface of the floor.

The Overseer took a step toward her and growled, blood dripping down his nostrils, "There is no going back!" He made as if to lunge at her, before being knocked sidewise against the sudden jerk of the ship. He tumbled, hanging there in the air, still, as the Troodon did earlier, before crashing down onto the rough floor of the *Chronus*.

Almost as soon as the Overseer crumpled, Gon'rak switched the ship back to its correct course, guiding the overheating laser to the previous spot on the asteroid. But the humming only increased in pitch, deafening the crew in the process. "*Chronus* is keeping course, how long is that laser of yours going to keep at it?"

In one way, the Overseer was correct, they needed to keep going if there was any chance to save their planet. But at least now, they were aware their fate, and now there was a choice. The others—the Overseer notwithstanding, since he was knocked out on the floor—seemed to agree in silence. Car'ren, however made the time to shoot Gon'rak a look of both thanks and disapproval before settling back into her station.

Tom'ras, the Twin on the left, was the first to respond, "The laser is almost through, if we want to keep at it, though I don't know if it will make it in time."

It was odd, Gon'rak thought. Inside the craft, the captain lay dead. Alarms blared, the thrumming continued, and he could almost feel the pounding heartbeats of everyone in the cabin. But on the monitor, the asteroid hung there, as if assured in victory. As if nothing they did or tried would prevent its inevitability.

Did they have any chance? Gon'rak felt as if he'd aged 20 years in the last 20 seconds. He felt wiser now, more mature, as the realization that they were unlikely to survive struck him. *I will pick a path and stick with it. I will stay this course and fulfill my duty, no matter how small of a role I have.*

"By the Two-Headed God!" A Twin exclaimed. "The laser is going to work. Just a little bit longer!"

"Great. Now what?" Gon'rak said, not convinced of their victory. The cautious way Car'ren was staring at her control panel, he wasn't sure of anything right now.

"Calculating the new trajectory of the asteroid if the laser succeeds," she said. "But Gon'rak, you went a little crazy back there, I'm not sure if we can accurately predict—"

"What?"

The thrumming stopped, and for a moment, the quiet was more alarming than the noise.

"Done, switching the laser off!" Tom'ras said in triumph.

There was a moment, where an eternity was suspended between Car'ren, the Twins, and the switch. Car'ren was stopped mid-sentence and one of the Twins placed their claw on the control. And in that moment, their world exploded, just as violently as he had witnessed the destruction of the moon and their home. The ship shattered where the laser was housed, where the coolant tank had been. It was just bits of strewn steel now.

"Seal the ship!" Car'ren commanded as time snapped forward again. He held to hope that the inner hull wasn't as badly damaged, and the shield dampeners could hold, or they'd all be dead. "Are fire suppressions engaging?"

"Some of them," came a reply from a Twin. Gon'rak didn't know which one. He was too busy figuring out which controls still worked. "Captain—Car'ren," he corrected, "I have minimal movement. Most of the flaps are still working, I can fly a little once we are in an atmosphere, but right now, we are just along for the ride."

"No, stay out of the atmosphere!" Car'ren cried, "Keep us out of there. We can't interfere with Earth if there is even the slightest chance we can return home." But her voice betrayed her hopelessness. She knew as well as anyone that the explosion was likely to have left them incapable of escaping Earth's gravitational pull.

"Would that I could," Gon'rak replied truthfully. He hated disappointing her, but this part at least, was outside of even his piloting ability, "The explosion pushed us right into orbit, we don't have enough power to escape it."

Car'ren looked over at her consoles, as if to confirm. As her head feathers lowered, Gon'rak could tell that she knew it was true. But it didn't matter. The ship began to feel hotter. The fog seemed to turn to steam before his eyes. Thunder roared outside the thin skin of the damaged hull. Earth had them within its grasp, and they were burning up in their descent.

Gon'rak twisted the controls. This was now his ship, the *Chronus* was under his control. He knew he was a better pilot than the primary he'd replaced at the last minute. Maybe he wasn't as educated, maybe he wasn't as obedient, but he was damned sure he could still maintain some control of the crashing craft.

But his arms were already weary from the resistance the controls had given him earlier. They felt like heavy bags of sand, and just lifting them was a chore. He tried to push the pain aside with what little strength he could muster. Besides, if he survived, he'd get to see the giants of the past, not fossils he'd seen hung in the museum. And maybe he'd get to see the moon whole. He could see it with Car'ren. That was worth fighting for.

Bursting through the clouds, the prehistoric blue world opened up before them. If he wasn't so busy keeping the free-falling ship from crashing into the green, Mesozoic mountains, he'd stop and stare out at the monitors. A stolen glance at Car'ren revealed she was doing just that. He smiled inwardly, until what little he did see showed him that the ground was rising to meet them. He punched the buttons for the different flaps, spreading them out, hoping for anything to increase their resistance and decrease their speed. There was some control over the thrusters, but they were burning out, becoming useless, as they expended the rest of their energy to slow the ship.

"It's not going to be a smooth landing, but we aren't going to crash," he paused, "too badly."

"What?" The cry came from Car'ren. One would have thought thanks were in order. Instead, she continued, "No," she continued, "We have to crash, we cannot change the timeline any more than we already have. Who knows what the ramifications would be?"

As soon as she asked, the back of the ship slammed into the soft foliage of the jungle canopy. Gon'rak got another burst from the thrusters, and raised the ship once more, but only for a moment. They jolted down again, this time deeper into the brush. The monitors all went blank, and it went dark in the control room. Anything bolted to the side of the ship was torn off by the trees. In between controlled crashes, Gon'rak became confused. Perhaps, under a less skilled pilot, they would have smashed into bits against the rocks and trees around them. But not him. So why was Car'ren yet again so disappointed?

Was she serious about not interfering? He could see himself living out the rest of his days on the rock outcroppings of the Cretaceous with her. It wouldn't be a bad life. Certainly, better than bursting into a ball of flame like he'd seen happen to Earth, hours ago. Only, it won't happen for another 66 million years… or not at all if they'd succeeded in knocking the asteroid off course. Time travel was confusing.

Chronus lurched forward, slamming abruptly to a stop. The Overseer was thrown into the air for a moment, and he landed hard against the floor once more. Gon'rak cheered a little to himself. But a moment later, the Overseer stood, apparently having been jostled awake by the fall. Before the Overseer could say anything, cracks appeared at the head of the cockpit. After a moment of stillness, the nose of the rocket cracked outward, spilling bright light into the otherwise darkened ship. Gon'rak shielded his eyes. The Overseer opened a hatch door.

"Get back inside, close that door!" Car'ren commanded.

"You forget your place, female." The Overseer said viciously through gritted teeth.

Before Car'ren or anyone could respond, several Troodons—their meals for the days ahead—sprinted for the openings. Gon'rak didn't blame the little feathery guys, but Car'ren seemed stressed. She darted out after one of them, shoving aside the Overseer as if he wasn't anything more than a bag of meat. She hollered through a series of deep hoots, "Get after them!"

Gon'rak didn't need to wait for an invitation to step outside. In his head, he was giddy. It was only as he stepped outside that he noticed one of the Twins was hurt. The two lay just at the exit, one nursing the other's wounds. He didn't even get a chance to look at the new world before he lost sight of Car'ren slipping off in between the thick trunks of the jungle trees. A moment later, the Overseer darted off after her. Gon'rak tried to look down at the Twins with concern, but he was worried for Car'ren.

"Go, Tom will be fine, I'll see to it. Then I'll determine if the ship can be saved." The Twin said, bobbing his head as if in doubt over either outcome.

Gon'rak too, bobbed his head in unspoken understanding, and went off after Car'ren, leaving the Twins behind.

As soon as the dense foliage surrounded him, there was the vaguest sense of seeing something familiar. Gon'rak stopped when something, a small creature he could barely see, dove into the underbrush. It looked like… Gon'rak thought hard about his museum trips with his mother. This jungle world looked nothing like the stark dry bones he'd seen. Everything here was humming with life. He thought of it. Could it be? Was this smaller creature, covered in dark brown quills and flat feathers, really be his ancestor? An *Acheroraptor*?

It didn't matter. The creature vanished and the jungle continued to close around him. He had to find Car'ren. A sick squeal a second later told him in what direction to go. He hurried ahead.

The jungle soon opened into a rocky clearing, high up on a hill. Everywhere else was dense foliage, except for what looked like a large body of water below the bluff. He could hear the waves from here. The breeze brought a taste of salt to his snout. And the sky was clear. Car'ren and the scene was altogether beautiful.

He saw what made the squeal. A bloody Troodon dangled from her teeth. In a smooth motion, she swallowed the small animal, feathers and all.

"Hungry?" Gon'rak asked mockingly, although something told him that wasn't the reason Car'ren ate the animal.

"You don't understand. We have to catch them all and destroy them…" Car'ren's voice trailed off before she finished, but she seemed to force the next words out of her, "And if we can't fix our ship we may have to destroy it and… ourselves."

Why? Gon'rak wanted to ask. But, before she could explain herself, there was a rumble from inside the foliage. Gon'rak thought it might be one of the critters he'd seen earlier. But instead, a low growl answered them in their tongue, "It's the first good idea I've heard yet, Car'ren. I'll happily start with the two of you." The Overseer stepped out onto the bluff, blocking their retreat. He was poised to pounce.

Gon'rak knew it was death for the Overseer. There was no way he could take on both of them and survive. But that wasn't the point. Raw anger seemed to drive him now. *And how badly injured would he and Car'ren come away from his attack?* His thoughts turned to her. The two of them could certainly kill the Overseer. But at what cost?

The Overseer took a step toward them, and the two of them stepped back, closer to the cliff. They'd have to spring forward now and attack him before they ran out of room. Car'ren raised her feathers high and prepped her toe-claws. Gon'rak did the same.

A chirping sound caught the three of them off-guard. As if on cue, they all cocked their heads sidewise in confusion. The critter that Gon'rak got a glance of earlier stepped out and mimicked them ticking its head sidewise too. The Overseer pivoted to this new threat, only to realize it wasn't a danger at all. Gon'rak thought it was cute.

"It's a raptor," he said. "One of us, only 66 million years or so removed."

But the Overseer didn't seem to care, he bared his teeth at the creature and let loose a reverberating growl.

"Careful, don't eat him, he could be your—"

The small raptor started to scurry away from the threat, back into the jungle. Suddenly, the Overseer lunged after it, as if instinct had fully taken over.

"Wait! What are you doing?" Car'ren called out. But it was too late. The Overseer vanished just as quickly as the raptor did earlier.

That's when the screaming started. The jungle shook violently. Gon'rak could hear snarls and the ripping of flesh. Feathers floated out through the trees. The Overseer screamed over the melee but moments later, the sound was silenced.

Gon'rak looked over uneasily at Car'ren, but she didn't have any answers either. The ocean was still at their backs below the bluff and the jungle stared out in front of them. Slowly, the raptor re-emerged from the jungle, its snout stained crimson. The ancestor clicked his claw-toe on the rock, as if in communication, and out slipped six others. They all began creeping toward the edge of the cliff to where Gon'rak and Car'ren were trapped like bait.

"I don't think this is going to work out any better than before."

"No, it's not." Car'ren grabbed his arm and spun him around.

"Are you doing what I think you are doing?"

"What's the use of feathers if you can't use them from time to time?"

"But we can't fly!" Gon'rak said, wishing he hadn't looked over at the steep cliffside below. The two jumped off the cliff.

Gon'rak found himself falling with his arms stretched wide and his feet tucked beneath them. Or, maybe he was flying, just as long as he didn't think about it too hard. He'd seen others glide before. But those were athletes who'd trained at it, like a sport. Gon'rak preferred to do all his aerodynamics inside a craft.

And, just like the *Chronus*, he was only controlling where he crashed. Even that was becoming less graceful than it sounded by the second. If his oversized talon didn't catch on a rock or a root, he thought he might be fine. But as the two descended, their speed picked up, until they were moving so fast, he knew neither one of them could control it.

Gon'rak couldn't help but hit the dirt. The abrupt friction flipped him, headfirst, and he landed heavily on his back, crushing his tail beneath him. He kept sliding down the steep hill, only this time, he could tell that he was slowing.

Finally, slippery gravel and rock gave way to thick, sandy beach, and his momentum all but gave out. He stopped, tasted grit, and tried to blow a bit of sand from his snout, only to find the wind knocked out of him.

But as soon as he was able, he checked on Car'ren's condition. She gave him a weary bob of the head, looked behind her, and said with some relief, "They aren't coming after us."

"Well," he breathed hard, looking up into the sky, "that's a good sign—" He froze.

As Gon'rak laid on his back he witnessed for the first time the giant asteroid—no, meteor now, he corrected, hanging above them in the sky.

And it was heading towards Earth.

* * *

The meteor hung low on the horizon, its shadow blotting out the sun, making it appear as if it were twilight. Gon'rak thought back again to what his father said. *Gods come when times are darkest.*

Only, it wasn't the shattered pieces of the Two-Headed God coming to rain down on them. It was their own hubris that would be the death of the planet this time. He thought back on the beginning of this journey that led him towards this moment and the sick pilot that he'd replaced.

It finally clicked. Gon'rak understood what Car'ren was saying all along. It wasn't just the meteor they wrought on the world. It was also what they brought with them. That was why they shouldn't have stepped outside the ship.

Disease. The bacteria and viruses that lived on them, on the Troodons, the same living organisms which made the pilot sick, were 66 million years in the making. There was nothing like it out here. The disease would spread as deadly as wildfire. *It was always the smallest things…* He understood that now. But it was already too late. What the impact of the meteor and its aftermath didn't wipe out, disease would certainly finish. They had doomed this world.

"I'm sorry." He said, slowly. The meteor kept falling.

Car'ren said nothing at first. Instead, she drew closer to him, and nestled her snout into the feathers on his chest. She felt warm. Optimism washed over him. *The world may burn, but our species might still somehow survive.* He held onto that belief. Perhaps the Acheroraptors would adapt and evolve in the wake of the meteor strike. And perhaps the diseases they had brought with them wouldn't be as deadly to their own kind.

Finally, she spoke, "We spent so much time killing each other and dividing ourselves. We never found a way to come together to accomplish anything significant. Maybe this alternate Earth will be better." It wasn't a question, but a hope.

Once again, Car'ren's words confused him. It wasn't what he was expecting. *What would this new world look like?* Before he could think on it further, from out of a hole near the sandy shoal, a furry mammal skittered away. He'd never seen a mammal before. They'd died out long ago. *I'm sorry, but it looks like you'll likely follow that same path in this timeline too*, he told the critter mournfully. But there was nothing for it now.

Off in the distance, he could hear the roar of a Tyrannosaur. It filled him with happiness. And in the sky, Pterosaurs swooped. It was then, looking skyward, that he caught sight of it. He'd never seen anything so magnificent before. He knew in the past, the moon was closer to Earth. How much closer, he had not realized until this instant. *And it was whole!* The moon, solid and bright, shone over them as the sky darkened. The Two-Headed God was gone.

Gon'rak was terrified and thrilled at the same time. He knew he would die, and what's worse, he knew he had helped destroy all that his kind had ever created. The moon gave him some comfort, just as it had all those years ago. Because whatever came next, he knew he could also take some solace that he, Car'ren and the Twins, creatures from a lost world, were privy to seeing the last twilight of the Mesozoic moon, unbroken as it was, before the new world swept them away.

End.

My friend and sometimes duelist Ricardo Victoria wrote a fascinating vignette about a *Velociraptor* landing on the moon. Neil Clawstrong, if I recall.

I immediately knew there was a story to tell here and I had to tell it. Long have we entertained the idea that, barring the meteor strike, some form of raptor-like dinosaurs (*Velociraptor* having long died out millions of years before the cataclysm) might grow into the dominant species on the planet due to their 'clever-girl' intelligence and pack coordination and just general coolness.

Twilight was a culmination of Ricardo's astro-dino-naught short piece and my story that set these dinos to new stars. Thanks, Ricardo, for making your sandbox big enough for the both of us. Twilight of the Mesozoic Moon went on to snatch a nomination for the Sidewise Award in alternate history in the Sidewise Award-winning *Tales from Alternate Earths* anthology.

I end with this, my favorite story to date, not just because it brought two of my deepest passions together: dinosaurs and time travel—

But because it helped forge a friendship.

Thank you for reading my collection of short stories. This book is the culmination of years of work, countless hours carefully pecking at a keyboard, and frustrating days of throwing out 99% of what I'd written to make something better with each new clack of a key.

Writing is one foot forward, two steps backward. On a high-speed treadmill.
That's on fire.

So, do me a favor and drop a line. Let me know what story you liked best. Let your buddy in on the secret. In fact, don't keep it to yourself. If you liked this book, let everyone know, including your favorite local bookshop.

While you're there, check out my other stuff. Order a copy if they're not on the shelves. Donate one to your library. Give one to your friend. Use a copy as a bribe for the troll who lives under the creepy bridge. You know the one.

About the Author

Brent A. Harris is a two-time Sidewise Award finalist of alternate history who writes about dinosaurs, fantasy, the fears of our future and the mistakes of our past.

When not writing speculative fiction, he focuses on his family, playing board games with friends, and talking nerdy. He holds a Master's degree in Creative Writing from National University as an NU Scholar. While he considers California his home, he currently resides abroad in Naples, Italy.

As of this printing, Brent is on his way to Okinawa, Japan where he will attempt to avoid the sweltering humidity, typhoons, and tangle of banana-spider webs for three frightful years.

If you enjoyed this collection of my stories, I urge you to read these books:

ALYX: An AI's Guide to Love and Murder

What if your home wanted you dead?
Tech-loving teen Christine makes fast friends with her home's AI, Alyx. But when a real-world romance threatens their bond, Alyx turns from friend to foe.

Alyx is a positive LGBTQ+ coming-of-age techno-thriller trapped inside a monster-in-the house horror where the home itself is the monster.

"...[Alyx] has elements of horror, romance, and great storytelling in general. It's a science fiction masterpiece that readers of all genres will love." *Jean-Paul Garnier, BuzzFeed News.*

A Twist in Time

Dickens Meets Steampunk.

Foundlings are disappearing from the workhouse where Oliver Twist once begged for a second bowl of gruel. He sets out to save them, with help from tinkerer, Nell Trent, and a slew of fantastical contraptions - including a mysterious pocket watch that allows its bearer to bend the rules of time. With Oliver's childhood nemesis, the Artful Dodger and her lethal bag of tricks dogging their steps, he discovers that there is more at stake than his own life and the missing orphans. Can he save London from the flames?

"Immersive worlds, fascinating characters, and gripping adventure!" *DJ Butler, author of Witchy Eye.*

"A thoroughly enjoyable romp through a steam-punk Dickensian London, with more than enough twists!" *--Tom Jolly, author of Ring Wave.*

A Christmas Twist: A Twist in Time Book II

A steampunk take on a Christmas classic.

Spirits, wronged by the greed of the living, descend on London. As Oliver Twist races across time to stop them, Nell Trent seeks revenge against the man who killed her: Ebenezer Scrooge. Can Oliver change the future or will the city succumb to vengeance? If you think you know this Christmas Carol, you're in for a Twist!

A Time of Need

Finalist for the Sidewise Award in alternate history.

In a change of fate, George Washington fights for the British and wrestles with his loyalties as he watches his countrymen struggle under the yoke of war. His nemesis, Benedict Arnold, seizes power and will stop at nothing to restore his family's honor by driving the British out of the colonies.

Far from the halls of power, the men and women in the army face difficult and painful decisions about their loyalty. Families are torn apart, and brother turns against brother.

"A Time of Need is an excellent novel in how a different personality commanding America's forces could have shaped the outcome of the American Revolution and the future path the young United States would have taken." - Matt Mitrovich, alternate history reviewer, *Amazing Stories*.

Thank you so much for reading! If you've made it this far, friend me on Facebook or follow me on Twitter or Instagram. You could leave a review on Amazon, I'd love that, but I'd love it even more if you took a pic of you reading this book or any of my others and posted it to social media. Tag me and let's see where we go! A writer can't survive on tears alone for long. We need hugs.

And whisky.